BUSTER BAYLISS
DAY OF THE HAMSTER

Polly was standing proudly in the middle of her bedroom. She had taken off her goggles, but you could see where they had been by the red goggle shape they had pressed into her face. She smiled smugly as Buster, Cole and Harvey came crowding in.

"It took a lot of brainwork," she explained, "but luckily, I've got a lot of brains. I've mixed up something that I hope will do exactly the reverse of whatever your mixture did."

"Is it that blue stuff in the jar on your desk?" asked Buster.

"Yes."

"'Cos the cat's eating it."

PHILIP REEVE

BUSTER BAYLISS
DAY OF THE HAMSTER

ILLUSTRATED BY STEVE MAY

■SCHOLASTIC

Scholastic Children's Books,
Euston House, 24 Eversholt Street,
London, NW1 1DB, UK
a division of Scholastic Ltd
London ~ New York ~ Toronto ~ Sydney ~ Auckland
Mexico City ~ New Delhi ~ Hong Kong ~ Smogley

First published by Scholastic Ltd, 2002
This edition published by Scholastic Ltd, 2007

Text copyright © Philip Reeve, 2002
Cover and inside illustrations copyright © Steve May, 2007

Cheese supplied by the Spudsylvanian Dairy Produce Marketing Board.

10 digit ISBN 0 439 94291 8
13 digit ISBN 978 0439 94291 1

Printed and bound by CPI Bookmarque, Croydon, Surrey

10 9 8 7 6 5 4 3 2 1

The rights of Philip Reeve and Steve May to be identified as the author and
illustrator of this work respectively have been asserted by them in accordance
with the Copyright, Designs and Patents Act, 1988.

The noises described in this book were developed specially at Scholastic Ltd's
top-secret sound effects testing range in the Nevada Desert. Do NOT try to
recreate them at home.

Paper used by Scholastic Children's Books are made from
wood grown in sustainable forests.

1. Hamish the Hamster and the No Pet Promise

"Aaaaargh!" wailed Buster Bayliss, as he so often did. "No! Not that! Anything but that! Have mercy!"

"But Buster," said Miss Ellis patiently, "it's your turn. Everybody else has looked after Hamish for a weekend. Now it's your go."

Resistance was futile. Buster slumped across his desk and made a hopeless, doom-laden, moany noise*. He could distinctly remember his mum making him promise never ever EVER to bring a school pet home for the weekend again. Ever. She just didn't understand that when you were at school you sometimes *had* to take turns looking after the class gerbil, or the class terrapin, or, in Hamish's case, the dozy class hamster.

Mind you, she had a point. Buster's house seemed to be a sort of death-trap for school pets. He could imagine mother and father school pets threatening their children with it – "Come on son," they'd go, "eat up your sunflower seeds/ants' eggs/gerbil food, or we'll make you go and spend a weekend at BUSTER BAYLISS'S HOUSE!"

It wasn't that Buster actually set out to harm the poor creatures. He liked animals, and was always careful to feed them properly and fill up their water bottles and provide them with everything that a goldfish, rat or rabbit could possibly need. It was just bad luck. Wearily, Buster remembered the long list of unlucky pets he had taken home for the weekend. There had been Minnie the gerbil, who had eaten Mum's favourite jumper and then had to be rushed to the vet with a severe case of jumper-poisoning. There had been Bartok the Goldfish

* "Ooooooooooohhhhhhhh," it went.

2

(sprained tail), Chloe the Chinchilla (appendicitis), Norman the Guinea Pig (earache) and Russell the Rabbit (who turned out to be a girl, and had baby rabbits all over Mum's new sofa). All of them had needed expensive trips to the vet as soon as they set foot or fin over the threshold of number 21 Ashtree Close. Poor Edna the Stick Insect hadn't even made it through the door; she had spontaneously combusted as Buster carried her tank up the front drive, and it had taken a whole team of vets working overtime to save her.

"Right," said Mum, after that. "That's it. These school pets are more trouble than they're worth. I'm sick and tired of spending my Saturdays queuing up at the vet's surgery and paying for splints and pills and bandages for animals that aren't even mine. You're not to bring any more of them home for the weekend, Buster, understand?"

She had even given him a letter to give to Miss Ellis, explaining why, but Buster had forgotten all about it, and it had been kicking about in the bottom of his school rucksack for months and months and months. He had a quick hunt for it now, as Miss Ellis advanced on him with Hamish, but he couldn't see it, and he didn't want to feel about in the perilous lower depths of the rucksack – who knew what might lie hidden down there, among the ancient choccy-bar wrappers and bits of fluff and long-lost items of PE kit?

"Oooooooooohhhhhhhhhhhh," he moaned again, as Miss Ellis dumped the smelly cage containing Hamish on his desk. He peered in through the bars. Hamish didn't look ill. He didn't look worried at the thought that he would soon be carried through the dread portals of the House of Doom. He was doing what he usually did, i.e. sleeping; all you could see of him was a little furry tummy rising and falling amid the sawdust.

"Stupid hamster!" muttered Buster, as Miss Ellis went back to her desk. "I don't know why people think hamsters make good school pets. They just snooze all the time, so you never see them. You might as well keep a furry pencil case in a cage and call it Hamish. . ."

"Well, I think he's cute," said Linzi Moss, who sat at the next table.

"Why don't you take him for the weekend, then?" Buster suggested eagerly. "I mean, it'll be a terrible disappointment for me, but I'll get over it, time is a great healer. . ."

"Not flippin' likely!" said Linzi. "Last time I had him at home he ate my dad's slippers and I ended up with my pocket money stopped for a month."

"Oooooooooooohhhhhhhhhhhh," said Buster.

When the bell went at the end of the afternoon Buster was usually the first out of Crisp Street Middle School. But not today. Today he trudged along at the rear of the army of escaping children, weighed down by Hamish and Hamish's cage and Hamish's overnight bag and Hamish's bulging bag of Hamish-food. "Why I have to carry your food for you I'll never know," he grumbled grumpily. "I thought you did that sort of thing for yourself. I thought you carried it in your cheeks. What's the point of being a hamster if you have to make somebody else carry your nosh about for you? That's what I'd like to know. . ."

"Talking to yourself, Buster?" asked a voice. It was the sort of voice that sounded as if it wore glasses and scored 11 out of 10 in surprise spelling tests, and sure enough, when Buster made a gap in his pile of hamster-things and peered through, he saw his Fake Cousin Polly trudging along beside him, dragging her enormous tuba case behind her.

"Actually," said Buster, "I was addressing Hamish the Hamster."

"Coo!" said Polly. "Can I have a look?" Before Buster could object she had grabbed Hamish's cage and was going, "Ahhhhh! Look! What a cute little furry tum! Can we wake him up?"

"Don't you dare!" warned Buster. "Let sleeping hamsters lie, that's what I say. If you wake him up he'll start running round and round in that little wheel of his and he'll probably fall off and break his ankle or something and my mum will get lumbered

with another trip to the vet. Or he'll work up an appetite, and as soon as I get him home he'll eat something he's not supposed to. It was bad enough having school pets home when she was just a lollipop lady, but now she's presenter of Britain's third most popular TV archaeology prog and she's got all sorts of scripts and papers and faxes and important books lying about at home. If Hamish eats those, she'll kill me!

"Actually," he went on gloomily, "she's probably going to kill me anyway."

Polly ignored him. "Hello Hamish!" she cooed, gently tapping the underneath of the cage. "Wakey wakey! Who's a cutesy-wutesy little hammy-wammy-spimmy-spammy then?"

"Don't call him that!" wailed Buster. "You'll embarrass him! You might embarrass him so much that he *dies* of embarrassment and then I'll have to take him back to school in a shoebox on Monday morning and Miss Ellis will kill all the bits of me that Mum hasn't already killed for bringing him home in the first place. . ."

Hamish, dimly wondering what all the noise was about, opened one sleepy eye, then closed it again and rolled over. "Zzzzzzzz," he said.

"Ahhhhh!" purred Polly. "Look! He opened his little *eye!* Isn't he *clever!*"

"Just leave him alone, Polly," Buster pleaded. "I can't hang about here all afternoon. All these bags and boxes weigh a tonne!"

"Oh, poor Buster!" said Polly. "Would you like a lift home with all this stuff?"

Buster peered past her to where her mum's car was waiting in the street outside the school gates. It was a super-ginormous 4x4, bigger than most people's houses, and there would easily be space inside for Buster and all his hamster-related baggage. Snug in the back seat, he would be back at Ashtree Close in about two minutes. It was tempting. Unfortunately, Polly's mother was Fake Auntie Pauline, Mum's oldest friend, and she probably knew all about his "no pets" promise. Even if she didn't, she'd be sure to mention Hamish next time she rang Mum up for one of their four-hour chat-a-thons, and Buster was still sort of hoping that he might be able to smuggle the hamster in and out of the house without Mum ever knowing.

"It's all right," he sighed. "I'll walk."

And so he walked, an enormous heap of bags and boxes with a hamster on top, ambling along on two scruffy legs. By the time he reached the end of Crisp Street and came out into Dancers Road he was so weary that he knew only chocolate could save him. He popped into the newsagent's for a bar of the gooey, minty-centred sort, and it was while he was standing outside, guarding his pile of hamsteriana and gloomily munching that he noticed the notice.

It was a smallish, dirtyish notice, and it was stuck to the inside of Mr Kumar's shop window with three blobs of Blu-tack and a bit of bubblegum. It said:

PROFESHUNNAL
PETT MINDING SERVISS

Out at work all day?
Going away for the week?
Or simply bored with your pett?
Whatever the reezon,
we'll care for your pett
in luckshery at

THE PETZ
4-STAR PETT HOTEL!
NO 24, PIECROFT VILLAS

Only 75p per night!
Discount rates for groop bookings.
No dinosaurs or big scary spiders.

It all looked very professional to Buster. In fact, it might just be the answer to all his problems. And he was sure he had heard that address somewhere before, although he couldn't think where. Maybe

Polly had mentioned it – the Petz sounded like just the sort of place where Fake Auntie Pauline would leave her huge and horrible cat, Fluffikins, when she and Fake Uncle Tim zoomed off on one of their posh holidays.

Luckily, it wasn't very far to Piecroft Villas. Five minutes later Buster was ringing on the doorbell of number 24, which was a strangely familiar-looking house, and about twenty seconds after that it was opened by a tall, pretty, kind and familiar-looking lady who said (in a very familiar voice), "Sorry, but I didn't order an enormous pile of bags, boxes and hamster on legs. . ." Where *had* he met her before?

"I'm here about the pet hotel," explained Buster, peering plaintively at her through the tiny chink between Hamish's cage and Hamish's spare-sawdust bucket.

"Pet hotel?" The lady frowned. "I'm sorry, I think you've got the wrong address, this isn't a—"

"Mum, Mum, Mum, it's all right, Mum!" shouted two voices from somewhere behind her, and there was a scrambly, clattery sound of computer games being flung aside and be-trainered feet thundering down stairs. "It's for us, Mum! We'll deal with this! You go and have a nice sit down and a cup of tea. . ."

Two boys pushed past her and stood beaming at Buster. "Welcome to the Petz!" they chorused.

Buster looked them up and down, from their tousled hair to their muddy trainers, and realized why their house and their mum had seemed so hauntingly familiar — it was because he'd spent half the summer holidays round here playing computer games and mucking about in the garden. They weren't the owners of a luxurious 4-star pet hotel at all! They were the Quirke Brothers.

2. A REALLY BAD iDEA

"What's all this about a pet hotel?" asked Mrs Quirke suspiciously, grabbing each Quirke brother by an ear and lifting them up on to the tips of their trainers. "This isn't another one of your hare-brained get-rich-quick schemes, is it?"

"No, Mum," said Harvey Quirke.

"No, Mum," promised his younger brother, Cole.

"Because you remember what happened last time," said their mum. "When you tried to market your patent hair-restorer. . ."

"Yeah," said Harvey angrily. "Dad still hasn't given us the 50p for that bottle he bought off us."

"I'm not surprised!" said Mrs Quirke. "He couldn't go out for a month! He still has to wear a hat!"

"I don't know why he made such a fuss about it," muttered Cole. "It made his hair grow back, didn't it?"

"Oh, it grew back, all right," agreed Mrs Quirke. "But two metres long, and pink!"

"I thought that was very good look for Dad," said Harvey. "Anyway, we've given up all that sort of thing."

"Honest," said Cole.

"Hmmmmm." Mrs Quirke looked them up and down, not taken in for a second by their innocent expressions. She pointed at Buster. "Then why is there an enormous pile of bags and boxes with a rodent on top standing on the front door step?"

"Oh, that's nothing to do with any ill-advised attempts to earn extra pocket money," Harvey promised. "And it isn't going to go wrong and lead to disaster in any way. This is just a friend of ours. Buster. You remember Buster. He's popped round to . . . er. . ."

14

"To play Pet Hotels!" said Cole brightly. "It's this brilliant new computer game where you have a hotel and you have to look after it like it's a pet. You take it for walks and feed it and clean up after it, and if you don't do it properly it gets ill and closes down. . ."

"Yes, yes," Harvey agreed, "but if you do it properly it has lots of little baby hotels. That's where caravans come from. . ."

Mrs Quirke's eyes had taken on that misty, double-glazed look that mums' eyes do when you start explaining computer games to them. "Well, all right, I suppose," she said. "But I've got my eye on you two."

She went back inside the house.

"Phew!" said Harvey.

"Phew!" agreed Cole.

"Here," said Buster, "how come you two muppets are running a pet hotel? I thought you were supposed to be fearless monster hunters?"

"Nahh," said both Quirkes together. Harvey explained. "The bottom's dropped out of monster hunting. Very hard to make a profit these days. High overheads, long hours, lots of rules and regulations. . ."

"Plus you sometimes have to hunt monsters," said Cole. "And it's really scary!"

"So we decided to go into pet minding," explained Harvey. "We just have to look after people's pets for the weekend, and we get paid 75 whole p per day! We made a few rough calculations and we reckon we'll be multi-multi-multi-quintillioniares by the time we leave school." He peeked into Hamish's cage. "So this is the little chap you want us to take care of, is it?"

"Errrrr, ummmm, yes," said Buster, even though he was getting frantic messages from his brain saying, *"This is a REALLY, REALLY BAD IDEA!"*

"Shut up, brain," he told it.

"All right," said his brain. *"But you'll be sorry. . ."*

Buster knew what his brain meant. Ordinarily, he wouldn't leave the Quirke Brothers in charge of anything, let alone a valuable school pet. On the other hand, if Hamish didn't stay with them, he would have to come home to Ashtree Close, and Mum was almost sure to notice. . .

"All right," he said. "I want to leave Hamish in your hotel until Monday morning. But only if I can be ABSOLUTELY SURE that you know what you're doing. You *do* know what you're doing, don't you?"

"Oh, yes," said Harvey.

"Almost completely," said Cole, nodding so hard that he made himself dizzy and had to sit down.

"Your guinea pig will be perfectly comfortable with us."

"He's not a guinea pig!" protested Buster.

"Oh. . ." Harvey looked a bit perplexed and had another look at Hamish. "Er . . . gerbil? Chinchilla? Puppy?"

"Bee?" suggested Cole.

"He's a HAMSTER!" said Buster. "You've taken care of hamsters before, haven't you?"

"Loads," said Harvey.

"Quite a few," said Cole.

"Well. . ." Both Quirkes looked rather sheepish. "Actually, Hamish will be our first hamster guest," Harvey admitted.

"He'll be our first guest of any sort," added Cole. "Except for Auntie Ellie's budgie. But Harvey says we mustn't talk about what happened to Auntie Ellie's budgie."

"Shhh!" shushed Harvey, nudging his brother. "Shut up! Mr Bayliss isn't interested in what happened to Auntie Ellie's budgie. . ."

"Why?" asked Buster, a bit worried now. "What *did* happen to Auntie Ellie's budgie?"

"It wasn't our fault," Cole said. "We just thought he'd be lonely, all on his own in the hotel, so we put next door's cat in with him to keep him company while we went to watch *Buffy the Vampire Slayer*."

"Just a misunderstanding," said Harvey, busily trying to gag Cole. "Could have happened to anybody, Mr Bayliss. Nobody told us about that whole cat/budgie thing."

"It took Tweetie three whole weeks to stop shaking," said Cole, undeterred by the fact that Harvey was now sitting on his head. "He was so scared that all his feathers dropped off."

"Don't worry about a thing," Harvey promised, looking as confident and businesslike as it's possible to look when you're sitting on someone's head. He reached out to relieve Buster of the hamster cage. "Why don't you follow us through to the back garden, and we can show you round our state-of-the-art pet-care facility."

Buster was glad the Quirke Brothers had told him he was looking at a state-of-the-art pet-care facility, because if they hadn't he might have thought it was just an old potting shed. It stood half-forgotten at the overgrown far end of their long back garden, and seemed to be sinking like a torpedoed ship into a sea of mallows and thistles. The sagging door was tied up with string, but after a bit of fumbling Harvey and Cole undid the knots and let Buster look inside. He saw some shelves, mostly empty, except for a cluster of old bottles and jam jars on the top-most one.

There was a nice soft light from the dusty window, and a nice fresh breeze blowing through a hole in the wooden wall, and Buster had to admit that it looked like the sort of place where a hamster ought to be happy for a couple of days.

"We'll feed and water him regularly," promised Cole.

"Yes, and we'll come in for an hour in the morning and an hour in the afternoon and let him run around on the floor a bit," vowed Harvey.

"OK," agreed Buster. He put Hamish's cage down on a couple of old breeze blocks which the Quirke Brothers found in a corner of the shed, and filled the water bottle, and showed the Quirkes the food he had brought with him. He explained how much Hamish would need and how often his sawdust would need changing. Then he signed Hamish's name in the visitors' book.

"That'll be one pound fifty, please," said Harvey, holding out a grubby hand.

"One pound fifty! We're going to be rich! Rich!" cackled Cole, bouncing out into the garden and doing a gleeful little dance.

"Not so fast," Buster told them. One pound fifty was nearly five whole Mars bars' worth, and he wanted to be sure the Quirkes would do a good job before he started handing over that sort of money.

"I'll pick him up on Monday on my way to school," he said. "You can have your money then, just as long as nothing's gone disastrously wrong."

"Fair enough," said the Quirkes, who looked a bit disappointed but could see there was no point in arguing.

Buster knelt down to say goodbye to Hamish. "I hope you have a nice time," he said. "And please don't get ill or escape or eat anything that disagrees with you, 'cos you'll land me in terrible trouble. . ."

"ZⅢⅢⅢⅢ,"

said Hamish.

When you were kneeling down at hamster-level the breeze coming through the hole in the shed wall felt quite strong, and it suddenly made Buster afraid that Hamish might catch a chill or something. He rummaged about in his bag for something he could use as a draught excluder, and pulled out a limp, grey, pungent object. At first he wasn't sure what it was, but a quick sniff reminded him. "Eww! Argh! Ackgk!" It was one of his football socks. He quickly wodged it up and stuffed it into the hole. Not only did it keep the draught out, it filled the whole shed with a musty, fusty, cheesy sort of smell that he thought a holidaying hamster would probably enjoy.

Then he shouldered his school-bag and went out into the garden to join the Quirke Brothers, slamming the shed door behind him. He felt the happy, carefree feelings of someone who has had a great weight lifted from their shoulders. Now he wouldn't have to worry about smuggling Hamish in past Mum, and he wouldn't need to bother looking after the dozy rodent. The Quirke Brothers would make their one pound fifty and he could look forward to a lazy weekend spent watching telly and maybe biking down to the park for a game of Busterball. "See?" he told his brain. "What did I tell you? The Quirke Brothers may not be rocket scientists, but even they should be able to look after a hamster. Nothing can possibly go wrong. . ."

Meanwhile, something was going wrong. The jaunty way that Buster slammed the door shut had caused the whole shed to shake, and some of the jam jars on the top shelf fell over. The lids came off, and fluids spilled stickily out, yellow and purple and green, mingling together to form a gloopy brown puddle that smouldered a little as it oozed towards the edge of the shelf and began to

DRIP

PLIP

DRIP

PLIP

PLIP

PLIP

down into the hamster cage beneath.

3. GROWING PAINS

Buster's happy mood lasted all through his walk home, all through tea (fish fingers and waffles, hooray!) and all through *I'm a Fading Celebrity, Get Me On Telly*. It survived a bath, and it was still there when he turned his bedside light out at 9 o'clock and snuggled down under the duvet and drifted off to sleep, planning a nice long weekend of mucking about.

Then, around midnight, it suddenly vanished.

"AAAAAAAAAAAAAAAAAAAARGH!"

he went, sitting rigidly upright in bed and screaming as quietly as he could so as not to wake up Mum. "What have I done? I've left Hamish with the Quirke Brothers! How could I have been such a pilchard? I'm DOOMED!"

He didn't get much sleep the rest of that night. He was too busy imagining all the things that might be going wrong round at the Quirkes' place. *What if they don't feed him? What if they feed him too much? What if his water runs out? What if that cat from next door breaks into the shed and scoffs him?*

But gradually all these small worries were eclipsed by one great big worry; a sock-shaped worry. He kept remembering the football sock he had used to plug that crack. Like all Buster's socks, it had been pretty ripe: Mum was always reminding him to put his PE stuff in the laundry basket on a Tuesday night, and he was always forgetting, so that sock probably hadn't been through a washing machine since last term — maybe even the term before! Personally, Buster didn't mind the smell; as long as you didn't get too close it was really rather sophisticated, a bit like that expensive foreign cheese Mum bought from the delicatessen at Christmas-time. But what if Hamish wasn't used to such rich odours? What if the cheesy foot-whiffs proved just too much for his little hamster nose? What if, even now, he was being suffocated by sock-fumes?

Buster was downstairs before Mum next morning, hoovering up his breakfast before she had even got out of bed. "Just going out to the hamster, I mean park," he shouted up the stairs, as he threw his empty Choc-o-Plops bowl into the sink for the washing-up fairies to take care of.

"But Buster, it's barely eight o'clock!" complained Mum, who had been enjoying a nice lie-in, but the only reply she got was the sound of the front door slamming.

It was one of those quiet, still, autumnal mornings when the fog hangs thick and white in the valley of the River Smog. Through the ghostly streets of Smogley a strange noise echoed, waking sleepy Smogleyites from their Saturday lie-ins. *Pladge pladge pladge pladge pladge pladge* **pladge pladge pladge** *pladge pladge pladge pladge*

25

it went. It was the sound of Buster's frantic footsteps as he sprinted through the silent streets, all the way from Ashtree Close to Piecroft Villas.

Pladge **pladge pladge pladge**
pladge pladge pladge screeeeeeeeeep!

He screeched to a halt outside number 24, long black skidmarks drawn along the pavement behind him, wisps of smoke uncoiling from the soles of his trainers. He hammered on the door and rang the bell until at last a sleepy-looking man with pink hair peered out through the letter box and said, "Yes? What?"

"I've got to see Harvey and Cole!" Buster explained breathlessly. "It's a matter of life and death and hamster!"

"Hah!" The letter box clanked shut, but just as Buster was getting ready for another assault on the doorbell he heard Mr Quirke stomping away into the house shouting, "Harvey! Cole! One of your weird little friends is here to see you!"

Shortly afterwards the door opened to reveal the Quirke Brothers themselves, bleary-eyed and Star Wars pyjama-d. "Buster?" they chorused, seeing the wild look on Buster's face. "What's wrong?"

"GottacheckonHamish!" Buster gasped, pushing past them and tearing through their house like a small whirlwind with messy hair.

"He's all right," Harvey and Cole both assured him, following him out through the back door and into the garden. "Look," they said, as they approached the shed. "The door's still shut; he'll be fine in there. . ."

"Oh no!" moaned Buster. That tightly shut door might have sealed Hamish's fate, trapping him in inside with the sockacious odours. He fumbled with the damp string and finally succeeded in undoing the knot. "Hold your noses!" he warned the Quirke Brothers, as he heaved the door open. . .

But he needn't have worried. There was a bit of an odd smell in the shed, it was true, but there was still plenty of air, and Hamish was sleeping peacefully in his cage.

"Satisfied?" asked Harvey. "Can we go back to bed now?"

"And is it safe to stop hoding our doses?" asked Cole.

Buster was so relieved that he had to sit down for a bit. He looked gratefully at Hamish's furry tummy as it rose and fell, rose and fell amid the sawdust.

That was when he first began to notice what was happening.

"Hang on!" he said. "He's got bigger!"

"He can't have," said Harvey.

"Can he?" asked Cole.

Buster put his nose against the bars of Hamish's cage and peered inside. Hamish had always been a podgy sort of hamster, but surely he never used to be quite this enormous? Yesterday he had been about the size of a well-stocked pencil case; this morning he was more like a big furry balloon, and Buster didn't think he'd be able to fit into his hamster wheel any more.

"You must have overfed him!" he said.

"No!" protested Harvey.

"Not us!" agreed Cole.

"Burp!" said Hamish, and as he burped his whole body seemed to bulge and swell and expand. The cage creaked, bars bending outwards as the big, furry body pressed against them.

"Wow!" said Buster.

"Eeek!" said Cole.

"I suppose it might just be a touch of wind," said Harvey hopefully.

"A touch of wind?" shouted Buster. He was angry; mostly at himself, for being stupid enough to leave poor Hamish here. "That hamster's the size of a labrador! How am I going to explain this to Miss Ellis? We won't even be able to get him out of his cage!"

"Oh no," said Harvey softly.

"Oh no," said Cole, like an echo.

"What do you mean, 'Oh no'?" demanded Buster – but the Quirke Brothers weren't listening. They were both staring up at the huddle of fallen jam jars on the shelf above Hamish's cage, and at the gunge that had spilled from them.

"Oh no!" they both said again.

"What?" wailed Buster. "What is that stuff?"

"It's the leftovers from our hair-restorer experiments," said Harvey. "The jam jars must have fallen over. I bet some of the drips fell into Hamish's cage and he licked them up."

"You mean Hamish's going to turn out like your dad?" asked Buster, going weak at the knees as he imagined going back to school on Monday morning with a day-glo pink hamster.

"No," said Harvey. "The stuff that made Dad's hair go pink was just the final product, and he made us tip it all down the loo. The stuff in those jam jars was all the experiments we brewed up while we were trying to get the mix right. There was a pink one and a green one and a yellow one, but none of them seemed to do anything very interesting. . ."

Buster tugged his sock out of the gap in the wall and started mopping up the puddle on the shelf with it before any more of the potion could plop into Hamish's cage. "Well, they've all mixed together," he said. "You've just got one sludgy brown one, now." He

29

sniffed the soggy sock and reeled backwards, choking and spluttering, tears streaming from his eyes. "Phew!"

"Eeek!" wailed the Quirkes. "Is it poisonous?"

Buster flung the sock aside and shook his head, wiping his nose on the back of his sleeve. "No, my socks always have that effect, I should have remembered. Your potion doesn't smell of anything much."

"Burp!" said Hamish, slightly louder than before, and the bars of the hamster cage gave way with a series of musical plings and twonks as his body went through another spurt of growth. He clambered out of the wreckage and set to work eating the bottoms of Harvey's pyjama trousers.

"Oi!" shouted Harvey, trying to hop out of range. "Make him stop! I'll be charging extra for that!"

"Extra?" Buster could barely believe his ears. "What makes you think I'll be paying you at all?"

"Look, he's eaten nearly a whole Darth Vader!"

"Only because you let him slurp up your weirdy hamster-expanding potion."

"But we didn't know it expanded hamsters! It was an accident! It was. . ."

 **" Burp!** announced Hamish.

Buster dived out through the shed door, and Cole and Harvey flung themselves after him. Behind them the shed bulged and groaned and burst apart, and a rhino-sized hamster shook the roof off its head and started gnawing on the scattered fragments of the walls.

"We've got to stop it!" Buster said.

"But how?"

"Well, you mixed the stuff up. You'll have to make an antidote."

"What's an antidote?" Cole whispered.

"It's a sort of gazelle," Harvey told him.

"Make something that will turn Hamish back to normal hamster size!" Buster shouted.

The Quirke Brothers just gawped at him. "But we can't. We've used up all the chemicals in our chemistry set."

boomed Hamish.

4. FOLLOW THAT HAMSTER

Mr and Mrs Quirke were pottering about in their kitchen. They hadn't bothered looking out into the garden yet, so they hadn't noticed that a giant hamster had scoffed their shed and was now tucking into the fence. They were just sitting down to breakfast when the three frightened boys came tumbling in through the back door.

"Mum!" yelled Harvey. "Dad!"

"What is it?" asked Mrs Quirke.

Harvey hesitated. There are some things that are difficult to explain to grown-ups, and the fact that you've transformed someone else's hamster into a shed-eating monster the size of a small dinosaur is one of the toughest. Harvey frowned and bit his lip while he wondered how to break the news to them, then decided that it wasn't worth the effort. "Can me and Cole have a new chemistry set?" he asked instead.

"No," said his parents.

Buster pushed Harvey aside. "But Mrs Quirke," he said, "there's this giant hamster and it's getting bigger every second and I've got to take it back to school on Monday and I don't even think it'll fit through the classroom door. . ."

"That's nice," said Mrs Quirke, buttering another slice of toast.

"Mum, you've got to believe us!" wailed Cole. He grabbed her by the hem of her dressing gown and dragged her out into the garden, Harvey and Buster close behind. "There!" they all said triumphantly, pointing.

"Where?" asked Mrs Quirke.

Hamish was gone, leaving only a large hole in the fence to show where he had made his escape.

"What have you done to the fence?" demanded Mrs Quirke. "And the shed! You little horrors! I'm stopping your pocket money for a month!"

She stormed back inside, slamming the kitchen door behind her.

"Now we'll never be multi-gazillionaires," said Cole ruefully.

"And we'll never be able to afford another chemistry set," said Harvey. "And even if we could, I don't know how we'd mix up the right antelope to shrink Hamish with, and even if we did, we don't know where he's gone."

Buster left them moping and mooched back up the garden to examine the hole Hamish had gnawed through the Quirkes' fence. When he looked through it he could see a trail of crushed shrubs and flattened flower beds leading away through next door's garden and out through another demolished fence into the streets beyond. The sounds of cars hooting, skidding and crashing into each other came dimly through the morning mist from the direction of Dancers Road. "I'm going to be in *so* much trouble," he groaned.

"Go and get dressed," he shouted, running back to the kitchen door, where Harvey and Cole were starting to shiver in their jim-jams. "Then follow me.

We've got to stop Hamish before he does any more damage!"

It isn't hard to track a giant hamster. If you've ever done it yourself you'll already know the tell-tale signs to look out for: the massive footprints, the crushed cars, the trees gnawed off halfway up their trunks, the – SPLAT "Yuck!" – enormous hamster poos.

Buster wiped his trainers clean on the kerb and ran on. Hamish seemed to have been wandering aimlessly up and down the side streets which branched off from Dancers Road. The cars which had been parked nose-to-tail outside the houses

there were squashed and mangled, and the chorus of warbling and cheeping car-alarms had alerted their owners, who were staring out of their bedroom windows in dismay. A milk float lay on its side at the corner of Poskitt Parkway, leaking rivers of milk and yoghurt which the neighbourhood cats were eagerly lapping up. "It was a monster!" the startled-looking milkman explained to anybody who would listen.

"Came out of the fog at me! A great big hairy thing, like a bear or a mammoth or a. . ."

"Hamster?" asked Buster, running up to him.

"Don't be silly, lad; it was enormous!"

"Which way did it go?" asked Buster.

"Sorry, son, I didn't see; too busy trying to keep my milk float under control. . ."

Buster ran on. It seemed to him that Hamish's trail was veering towards the park. That was probably quite a good place to head for if you were a giant hamster; just think of all those nice trees and shrubs waiting to be scoffed! Buster took a shortcut through a back alley and ran out across the fog-damp grass. There was no sign of poo or footprints on these lawns, but perhaps Hamish had made for the wooded bits beyond the bandstand. . .

Suddenly a terrible, blood-curdling scream cut through the fog, coming from somewhere away to Buster's right. "Eeeeeek! Yikes! Help! Keep away! Mummy!" "Hamish?" Buster ran towards the sound, scattering sleepy ducks who had been snoozing on the edge of the park pond. Soon the skeleton shapes of swings and climbing-frames loomed out of the murk ahead of him and he realized that he was in the children's playground. "Hamish?" he yelled again.

There was a sort of whimpery, squeaky noise going on somewhere nearby. Buster crept cautiously towards it. A huge shape reared over him, making him yelp with fright, but it wasn't Hamish — just the ramshackle old park-keeper's hut, with Mr Crust, the ramshackle old park-keeper, perched on the roof. He looked pale and shaky, and his official park-keeper's hat had fallen off.

"Mr Crust?" asked Buster. "What are you doing up there?"

Mr Crust stopped his whimpery squeaky noise and made some wild flailing gestures with his litter-spiking stick. "Watch out, boy! There's a monster loose! I was just out spiking some sweet wrappers and it suddenly came at me out of the fog, a great big hairy grey thing with a terrible, ravening mouth. And the smell —!"

The whirr of approaching wheels made Buster look round just in time to see the Quirke Brothers come whizzing out of the fog aboard their mountain bikes. He leaped out of the way as they slammed on their brakes and fell off.

"'Ere, you boys, no bikes allowed in the playground!" Mr Crust shouted, but you could tell his heart wasn't really in it; all he really wanted to do was nip home and have a nice cup of tea.

The Quirke Brothers stood up and dusted themselves off, straightening their cycle helmets. "Have you seen Hamish?" Buster asked.

"He's over on the far side of the park, rootling about in the trees," said Cole, pointing.

"He can't be," said Buster. "He only came past here about two minutes ago."

"Tried to eat me!" called Mr Crust helpfully.

"It can't have been Hamish," said Cole firmly. "We've been keeping an eye on him for at least five minutes. Mr Crust must have been mistaken."

"Mistaken how?" asked Buster. "I mean, how many other dirty big hairy hamsters are rampaging around Smogley this morning?"

The Quirkes shrugged. "Come and see for yourself, if you don't believe us."

Buster climbed on to the cross-bar of Harvey's bike, and they set off, wobbling away from the playground and the petrified parkie and gathering speed as they passed the empty bandstand and went down the steep slope into the bit of the park known as the Dell. The Dell was supposed to be a Woodland Environment, but these days it was more of a Rubbish Environment, with old cars and fridges dumped among the trees and scraps of litter speckling the winding woodland paths. Today it looked scruffier than ever, because a great swathe of trees had been uprooted and flung aside, and in the midst of the wreckage lay a huge, hairy body. Monster-sized snores echoed from the slopes of the

Dell, and as Buster and his friends approached the sleeping hamster they could hear its tummy grumbling and wheezing like modern jazz.

"Brilliant!" Buster whispered. "He's gone back to sleep! That'll keep him out of trouble for a while."

"But what about when he wakes up?" asked Harvey.

They propped the bikes against a rusty fridge and crept closer. The hamster's vast flank rose and fell in time to its snores, and its pink nose twitched and snuffled. Huge whiskers jutted into the foggy air like radio masts, and two front teeth the size of garage doors hung above the boys. The Quirkes peered up at them from under their cycle helmets, looking like a pair of frightened mushrooms. "It wouldn't hurt us, would it?" said Cole nervously.

"Mr Crust said it tried to eat him," Harvey recalled. "But hamsters are vegetablarians, aren't they?"

"Normal hamsters are," whispered Buster. "But who knows about huge great monster hamsters what have been given dangerous chemicals to drink by a pair of lupins? They probably eat anything they can find, people included. That's why we've got to get hold of an antidote as soon as we can, and bring it back here before he wakes up."

"But we've got no chemistry set!" Harvey reminded him.

"Then we'll find someone who has. My Fake Cousin Polly. She's been top in science three years in a row. I bet she's got all kinds of chemistry sets and bunsen burners and particle accelerators and stuff round at her house. Come on."

They tiptoed back to the bikes. Buster knew that it was going to be embarrassing admitting to Polly what a mess he had got himself into – but not as embarrassing as having to explain a car-squashing, people-scoffing hamster to his mum and Miss Ellis. Perhaps, if Polly could help them devise an antidote, and they could get it back here before Hamish woke up, there was still a chance that the grown-ups would never work out what had happened. . .

5. THE CAT IN
THE HAT

Dancers Road was a scene of chaos and devastation as Buster and the Quirkes wobbled along it on their bikes, heading towards the posh end of town where Fake Cousin Polly lived. Actually, Dancers Road was usually a scene of chaos and devastation on Saturday mornings, when cars snarled up in a great big honking queue on their way to the out-of-town supermarkets. Today it was even worse. Police cars and fire-engines were pulling up with sirens shrieking and blue lights flaring through the fog. People were standing around scratching their heads and wondering why their cars were now only twenty centimetres high, while others stared in amazement at bent-over lamp-posts and ruined roofs. Near Buster's school a reporter from the local TV station was talking into a big microphone. Buster made the Quirke brothers halt their bikes, and heard her say, "I'm speaking live from Smogley, where a freak earth tremor earlier this morning has caused a lot of damage to property. With me is Mr Nutley Wagstaff, the Mayor of Smogley. Tell me, Mr Wagstaff, are you worried about the danger of aftershocks?"

"Not at all, Trixie," said Nutley Wagstaff, a round, beetroot-coloured sort of mayor with Brillo-pad eyebrows.

"And what about the reports we've been getting that the damage wasn't caused by an earthquake at all? Some people claim to have seen what can only be described as a great big hairy monster."

"Absolute nonsense, Trixie," chortled the mayor, looking shifty. "The situation here in Smogley is completely under control, and I hope this morning's little upset won't put your viewers off attending this afternoon's big event at Smogley Docks. . ." He leaned close to the camera, so that his huge red face reared up in all the television sets in the windows of the nearby electrical shop, startling the passers-by. "Remember, viewers," he said, "the fun starts at two thirty sharp, and at three the Smogley Docks Experience will be officially opened by our very special guest, actor Dwight Placebo, who plays lovely Dr Doug in top TV hospital drama *Lovely Doctors!*"

"What was he murbling about?" Buster asked, as they pedalled onwards. He'd heard of Dwight Placebo – Mum went all sigh-y and made him keep quiet whenever *Lovely Doctors* was on – but he couldn't imagine why a top TV star would be coming to Smogley.

"It's the official opening of the Smogley Millennium project, of course," said the Quirke Brothers. "Don't you know anything?"

"It's a bit late, isn't it? The millennium was ages and ages and ages ago."

"Well, they've only just finished it," said Harvey. "They've turned those old docks down on the canal-side all posh. There are coffee shops and art galleries and expensive flats and a visitor centre with dummies dressed up like old canal-workers and a model canal boat, and they're opening it this afternoon."

"There's going to be a giant furry seal," said Cole.

"A what?" scoffed his brother.

"That's what Mum said," Cole replied. "I asked what was so special about this Smogley Docks Experience thingy, and she said there was going to be a giant furry seal beside the canal."

"No she didn't!"

"Did!"

"Didn't!"

"Oh, stop bickering," snapped Buster. He had been jiggling up and down on the crossbar of Harvey's bike for nearly three kilometres, and it wasn't helping to improve his temper one bit. "This is no time to start worrying about giant furry seals. We've got a giant furry hamster to sort out . . ."

"Oh, *Buster!*" sighed Polly half an hour later, when Buster had finished explaining what had happened. "Can't you do anything properly?"

"It wasn't my fault!" Buster whined.

"It doesn't matter whose fault it is," Polly said wisely. "Something has to be done, and I suppose it's up to me to do it, as usual. You're lucky Mummy and Daddy are out at the shops this morning. Come on upstairs and we'll see what we can do . . ."

46

The Quirke Brothers chained their bikes up and then followed Buster inside. The front of Polly's house had been repainted recently, after an unfortunate exploding sprout incident, but everything inside was just the same; flowery wallpaper, knick-knack cabinets full of expensive knicks and even more expensive knacks, deep, soft carpets and bowls of smelly pot-pourri which made the Quirke Brothers sneeze. "Don't touch anything," Polly warned sternly, as the three boys trooped after her up the stairs and into her room.

They stood and stared about themselves in horror as she started hunting around in her chest of drawers. They had been in Polly's room before, but they'd been busy running from a man-eating sprout at the time and they hadn't stopped to take in just how weird it was. For one thing, it was tidy! You could see actual carpet on the floor, not just an ankle-deep swamp of old comics and bits of Action Man like a proper bedroom. Even Polly's desk was all neatly laid out with pens and pencils standing to attention in little pots and a homework timetable pinned to the wall above it. Worse still, where proper bedrooms had posters of Smogley United, Polly's had big pictures of soppy-looking ponies and her favourite boy bands.

"Ewwwww!" moaned Buster, Cole and Harvey, shuddering with embarrassment.

"Stop shuddering with embarrassment and come and help," said Polly, clearing the pencil-pots and trim piles of schoolbooks from her desk and plonking them into Buster's arms. She handed racks of test tubes and tubs of brightly coloured powders to the Quirkes and told them exactly where they should be set up, then tied back her hair, pulled on an apron and snapped big plastic goggles on over her glasses. *She looks like a proper scientist*, thought Buster, brightening up a bit. *I bet we'll have a giant-hamster-antidote whizzed up in no time. . .*

"Now," said Polly, "have you got a sample of whatever it is you've been feeding to poor little Hamish?"

Harvey opened his rucksack and Cole dived in headfirst and emerged again a few seconds later clutching a couple of jam jars with dried-out chemical crusts in their bottoms. "This was all we could find," he explained. "We got them out of the ruins of the shed."

"There was a lot more soaked up on one of Buster's socks," said Harvey, "but we couldn't find it. We could go back and have a look for it, if you like."

"No!" yelped Polly, who didn't fancy the idea of

getting close to Buster's socks, even under laboratory conditions. "No, I'm sure what you've got here will be enough for me to do an analysis. Pass me that box of litmus paper and my junior spectrograph, and keep quiet. . ."

Buster had never realized how long it took to analyse dangerous substances and come up with antidotes. If this had been telly, you would have seen a big close-up of Polly working, and then a clock saying "ten to ten", and then the clock would go blurry and when you could see it again it would say "twenty past midnight" or something, and Polly would look up from a beaker of bubbling gloop and say, "Gentlemen, I think it's working!" But unfortunately this was real life, where time passed in great slow waves and the silence was broken only by the rattle of Polly stirring things about in test tubes and the Quirke Brothers going,

"ATCHOO!" "AHHHH - Ka-Ka-CHOOFF!"

from the after-effects of the pot-pourri. Soon, Buster was so bored that he couldn't sit up straight any more and melted into a little puddle on the floor. He couldn't bear this endless, aching silence, which seemed to throb and pound inside his head until he began to worry that he would go mad long before Polly found the antidote. Try as he might, he could not stay silent another second. . .

"Polly!"

"Shhh!"

"Have you found it yet?"

"Give me a chance, Buster; I only started two minutes ago. This sort of thing takes time and patience."

"But I haven't got any patience!" complained Buster. "And we haven't got much time either. If we can't get the antidote into Hamish before he wakes up, who knows what he'll do?"

"Be quiet, Buster!" Polly warned, turning round and frowning at him through her goggles.

"And I'm really hungry!" Buster added.

"Me too!" said Harvey.

"And me," agreed Cole.

Polly gave an exasperated sigh. "There are biscuits and things in the kitchen, but don't eat them all. And close the door," she added, as the boys stampeded biscuitwards. "I don't want the cat getting in here and knocking things over. . ."

Down in the kitchen, Polly's fat and greedy cat Fluffikins watched suspiciously as Buster and the Quirke Brothers tugged the lid off the biscuit tin and rummaged about inside. Fake Auntie Pauline was keen on Healthy Eating and Roughage and things, so Buster had been bracing himself for hand-knitted oatmeal cookies, but luckily the biscuits in the tin were meant for visitors. Fake Auntie Pauline had stocked up on all the nicest sorts, just in case anybody thought she couldn't afford them. There were crunchy ginger biscuits and Jammie Dodgers, and even some of those de-luxe chocolate digestivey things with a layer of gooey toffee hidden under the chocolate. A few minutes of mad munching later, the three boys were staring at an empty tin and a table full of crumbs.

"The trouble with biscuits," said Harvey thoughtfully, "is that they're too small."

"Maybe we could make a big one!" suggested Cole. "What if we mixed up some more hamster-growing potion, only instead of putting it in a hamster we put it in a packet of chocolate biscuits?"

"We could have the biggest biscuit in the world! We'd be famous!"

"Stop it!" shouted Buster, before they could get completely carried away. "What are you two like? You've already unleashed hamster horror on Smogley, and now you're planning to crush the whole place under enormous biscuits! It would be a disaster! There would be crumb-quakes and choc-chip avalanches and things. No, we're going to destroy every last trace of your hamster-expander, just as soon as Polly comes up with an antidote. . ."

Right on cue, Polly shouted down the stairs. "Buster! Quirkes! I think I've done it!"

They knocked down chairs, up-ended the biscuit tin and scrambled over each other in their hurry to get back upstairs, with Fluffikins scampering podgily behind them. Polly was standing proudly in the middle of her bedroom. She had taken off her goggles, but you could see where they had been by the red goggle shape they had pressed into her face. She smiled smugly as Buster, Cole and Harvey came crowding in.

"It took a lot of brainwork," she explained, "but luckily, I've got a lot of brains. I've mixed up something that I hope will do exactly the reverse of whatever your mixture did."

"Is it that blue stuff in the jar on your desk?" asked Buster.

"Yes."

" 'Cos the cat's eating it."

"AAAARGH!"

Polly leaped across the room, but too late to stop Fluffikins slurping up the last of the antidote. The fat cat must have slipped past her while she was talking to the boys, and jumped up on to the desk without anyone noticing. As Polly grabbed him and dumped him unceremoniously back on the floor he licked the last smears of blue from his whiskers and peered up at her with a faintly hurt expression, as if to say, "What? What have I done?"

"Oh no!" groaned Buster. "It took nearly an hour to mix that lot up! Now we'll have to start all over again."

Polly shook her head. "It's all right; I took notes of what I was doing, so it will be easy to make more. I'm just worried about poor Fluffikins. I mean, I know we need to find out if the stuff works before we give it to Hamish, but I hate the idea of using Fluffy as a guinea pig. I don't believe in testing things out on animals. I was planning to test it on the Quirke Brothers."

"Burp!" exclaimed Fluffikins, and bristled like a startled loo-brush, so fluffed-up with surprise and indignation that it took them all a moment to realize he had shrunk slightly.

"BURP! BURP! BURP!"

"Quick!" shouted Buster, "do something, before he vanishes altogether!"

Polly grabbed Fluffikins by his collar, but in the space of a few more burps he had shrunk to the size of a mouse. He dropped free of the collar and scampered away between the legs of the Quirke Brothers and out through the open door. They heard his burps getting smaller and shriller as he jumped down the stairs, and they bundled out of the bedroom in pursuit. They caught up with him near the bottom, trapped on the edge of a stair which was suddenly too high for him to jump off. He was about the size of one of those furry caterpillars you find in the garden at the end of summer.

"Keep back!" warned Polly. "You'll step on him!" She picked him up, carefully gripping the scruff of his tiny neck between finger and thumb. "Oh, poor little Fluff! Mummy's always saying that he needs to lose some weight, but I don't think she meant quite this much. . ."

"BURP!"

agreed Fluffikins. Buster had met burlier beetles. Still, it was hard to feel very sorry for Fluffikins, who usually spent most of his time killing small birds and unsuspecting mice and voles. Now the mice and voles would have a chance to get their own back.

"Well, at least we know it works," said Harvey brightly.

"Give him some of the first potion," Cole said. "that might grow him back to ordinary size."

"There's none left," Polly explained. "I used the last few drops up when I was doing my experiments."

"Bicycle pump?" suggested Harvey.

"No," said Polly firmly. "I'm afraid we'll just have to leave him. If my observations are correct (which they almost always are) then the effects of your horrid brew will wear off eventually."

"You mean it's just temporary?" said Buster, relieved. "Well, what are we worrying about then? There's no need to bother mixing up more antidote and risking our lives trying to persuade Hamish to drink it. All we need to do is wait until the effects wear off and he shrinks back to normal!"

"Except we don't know how long that will take," Polly said, looking around for somewhere safe to put her micro-moggie. She opened the hall cupboard and pulled a cardboard box down off the top shelf. Inside, upside down in a nest of crumpled tissue paper, sat her mother's best hat; an expensive frilly number shaped like a UFO. The deep bowl of its crown, lined with scrunchy silk, made a perfect home for poor Fluffikins, and as Mummy only ever wore the hat on extra-special occasions Polly was sure he wouldn't be disturbed there. She put him carefully inside and replaced the hatbox in its space on the shelf, leaving the lid off so that he could breathe. Then she turned to the others, looking even more serious than usual. "I really think we'd better get some of my shrinking potion into Hamish as soon as we possibly can. He may be sleeping now, but he could wake up at any moment. . ."

"Nahh," said Buster. "Not Hamish. He can sleep for

hours and hours and hours. When we're at school he does nothing but snooze all day. I guarantee you he'll be piling up the zizzes for hours yet."

From somewhere outside came the long, slithering crash of a collapsing building, the wail of car alarms, the howl of sirens and a thunderous, earth-shaking roar. Polly ran to open the front door and they all peered out into the fog. The sounds seemed to be coming from a few streets away, in the direction of the big supermarket on Gidleigh Road.

"On the other hand. . ." said Buster.

"He's awake!" cried Polly. "And he doesn't sound happy!"

6. SUPERMARKET SWEEP

Polly quickly mixed up another jam jar full of antidote, screwed the lid on tight, and left a note for her parents, who she knew would be worried when they came home from the shops to find her missing – *Dear Mummy and Daddy, Please don't worry, I have gone out to play with Buster Bayliss and will be back for tea,* it said. Reading through it, Polly realized that Mummy and Daddy would be even more worried when they found out she was with Buster; it might have been better to put, *Dear Mummy and Daddy, Just nipped out to tackle a giant rampaging hamster.* But there was no time to rewrite the note, so she left it on the kitchen table, weighting one corner down with the empty biscuit barrel.

Then they were off, hurrying on foot along the leafy streets west of Acacia Crescent, the Quirke Brothers pushing their bikes so as not to leave the others behind. Ahead of them the foggy air was filled with the sounds of disaster, and now and then people went sprinting past them in the opposite direction, shouting things like, "It's huge!" or "Run for your lives!" or "We're all going to die!" — tell-tale signs of a monster on the loose.

Running out into Gidleigh Road they found their way blocked by a cluster of police cars. Uniformed policemen were turning traffic and pedestrians away, while others crouched behind their cars and peered nervously into the swirling fog. From the far end of the street came the unmistakable sound of a supermarket being demolished by something big and hairy.

Unnoticed amid all the confusion, Buster and his friends crept closer. Nutley Wagstaff was standing beside one of the police cars, talking angrily to the officers inside. "What's wrong with your men, Chief Constable?" Buster heard him demand. "Why haven't they rounded the creature up?"

"We have been trying, your worship," said the policeman. "We waved our arms at it and went 'Shoo!', but it just ignored us."

"Then it's time to stop being all nice and woolly and humane!" the mayor shouted. "Call in the army! Get me tanks and rockets and armoured cars and really big guns!"

"Ooh, I do hope you're not going to harm the poor thing," said the policeman, who was an animal lover.

"All right, get some of those darts they use for tranquillizing rogue rhinos as well; but if those don't work, I want the beast killed. People aren't going to go on believing my story about earth-tremors for long, you know. Whatever this animal is, we can't afford to let it disrupt our Millennium celebrations. We're already years behind schedule, and if we have to delay the opening of the Smogley Docks Experience again we might as well wait for the next millennium."

"They can't kill Hamish!" squeaked Buster, hiding with the others behind an overturned van. "They mustn't! I've got to take him back to school safe and sound on Monday!"

"Come on," said Polly. "Let's see if we can get to him before the army arrives. . ."

The Quirkes chained their bikes up and all four children crept nervously past the roadblock, crouching behind hedges and garden walls until the fog hid them from the watchful policemen. The closer they came to the supermarket the more signs of devastation they saw; the cars in the car park had been shouldered clumsily aside and lay piled on top of each other in heaps. A wire trolley rolled past, half-filled with someone's Saturday shopping. "It's heading for the cheese counter, destroying everything in its path!" wailed a girl in supermarket uniform, running out of the fog and quickly vanishing again.

The supermarket was a ruin, the roof torn off, the windows shattered, a huge chunk missing from the front wall. Fog swirled eerily along the deserted aisles, and beyond it something vast heaved, turned, and vanished again.

"I didn't know hamsters ate cheese," Harvey hissed.

"SHHH!"

said everybody else.

Polly clutched her jam jar like an antidote-grenade, and they tiptoed towards the place where the hairy thing had been, crunching over broken glass and drifts of crisps, squelching through puddles of soup and lakes of custard and orange juice. They passed a super-de-luxe pedal car, the sort of thing a really spoilt three-year-old might get for Christmas, which had fallen off a high-up display stand and now lay up-ended in a mound of pasta shapes. In the electrical department a few upturned televisions blinked and fizzed, and on one of them they saw the Mayor of Smogley being interviewed again, beaming as he explained that everything was under control and invited everybody to come and join the fun at Smogley Docks that afternoon.

They knew when they had reached the cheese counter, because there was a big sign saying, *"CHEESE COUNTER"* and then another saying *"Try our lovely selection of cheeses from around the world. THIS WEEK'S SPECIAL: Spudsylvanian Stinkhorn; the smelliest cheese on the planet!"* But that was all. There was no cheese to be seen, no counter, no hamster, not even a floor; just a gaping hole where something had burrowed its way into the earth beneath the supermarket. Buster ran to the edge of the hole and looked down. Eight metres below, water ran along a brick-walled tunnel.

"The sewers!" he said. "It's using the sewers to move about!"

"That doesn't sound very hamster-y," said Polly. "More like a rat..."

"And look!" Harvey pointed at the ragged edges of the hole, where a cluster of monster-sized hairs had got caught. The hairs were grey and shiny, nothing like Hamish's soft, biscuit-coloured fur.

"Maybe when Dad flushed our potions down the loo some of them got mixed together and a rat ate them!" said Cole, his teeth beginning to chatter. "Maybe we aren't just dealing with a giant hamster! Maybe we're facing a giant rat as well!"

"Well, whatever it is," said Buster, holding his nose, "it's done a great big cheesy fart."

"I'm not surprised," said Polly. "It's eaten a whole cheese counter. I expect you'd do cheesy bottom-burps if you'd just scoffed a few hundred tubs of extra-mature Spudsylvanian Stinkhorn. Mummy brought some of that home last week, and it really honked."

But Buster was not sure that the cheese was entirely to blame. He was thinking back to the park, and Mr Crust's encounter with a monster in the fog. "A great big grey thing", the park-keeper had said, and Buster had thought at the time that that was strange, but had just assumed Mr Crust must be colour-blind. But there had been a smell there too; a lingering, cheesy odour just like this, long before the creature could have eaten any Spudsylvanian Stinkhorn. . .

Ideas began to collide inside his brain, and a horrible suspicion started to form.

"I'm going down," he said.

"What?"

"I think there's something far worse than a giant hamster lurking down there, and I've got to deal with it. You lot can stay here, if you want."

"OK," said Harvey.

"Fine by us," agreed Cole.

"Don't you dare!" Polly growled, grabbing them by their collars and shoving them after Buster towards the edge of the hole. "You two caused this mess, and you're going to help Buster and me clear it up!"

They scrambled down the steep sides of the pit, holding on to the broken ends of girders and the spouting stumps of water pipes which jutted from the rubble. Soon they were standing up to their knees in the chilly water of the sewer, peering into the blind gloom of the tunnel. In the blackness something moved; they heard a furry body scrape and whisper against the dank brick roof.

"It's there!" whimpered Harvey.

"It's coming!" squeaked Cole.

The water churned white in the dark of the tunnel as a huge shape turned and came rushing towards the frightened children. Ahead of it it pushed a wall of fetid air, a disgusting, cheesy stink that made Buster fear he was going to faint. He saw a grey, close-woven hide and a shapeless, toothless mouth opening on blackness, letting out a hurricane of stinking cheesy breath and a terrifying roar which echoed and boomed in the narrow tunnel, shaking down loose plaster from the roof and bringing small avalanches of grit and debris tumbling down the sides of the hole.

"RUN!"

shouted Polly. Harvey and Cole were running already, scrambling up the sides of the hole and stopping, holding out their hands to haul the others up. Polly reached towards them, but Buster knew he had only one chance to use the antidote. He snatched the jar from Polly and hurled it towards the monster's gaping mouth, but missed. The jar shattered, splashing precious antidote uselessly over the tunnel wall. In another instant the horrible soggy fur of the monster covered him, squashing him down and threatening to squeeze the air out of his lungs, but small hands grabbed his flailing arms and dragged him clear, and he felt himself shoved and tugged and pushed and pulled and manhandled up the sides of the hole, while the great grey beast roared its fury behind him.

"What *was* that?" panted Harvey, when they were

all crouched shivering behind the bakery counter.

"It wasn't a rat," said Polly, who was good at natural history and knew about these things. "Unless it was some kind of mutation. It didn't have teeth, and it didn't have legs, and it didn't have eyes, and its pelt looked more like knitting than fur. . ."

Buster groaned. All his worst fears had been confirmed. "I know what it was," he said. "I've seen it before. It's one of my socks!"

DANGER!
SMELLY CHEESE
HAZARD!

7. KING PONG

"But that's impossible!" said Polly. "Socks don't destroy supermarkets! Socks don't attack people! I've never, ever heard of anyone being attacked by a sock!"

"You have now," said Buster weakly. "I recognized it at once. That big raggedy mouth is the hole where my toes used to stick out."

"It must be the one you used to mop up the spilled potion in the shed," said Harvey.

"That's really cool!" said Cole. "Our formula doesn't just make things grow to giant size, it brings socks to life! We could keep a few in captivity on an island somewhere and people would pay lots of money to come and look at them! It would be like *Jurassic Park*, but with socks."

Buster shook his head. "I don't think it was brought to life by your potion," he said. "I think it was alive already. I always wondered where my socks went to. This probably isn't the first; it's just the others stayed normal size, so I never noticed when they sneaked off. It's ages and ages since I remembered to wash my PE socks, and I wear them most weeks, and the rest of the time they just sit down there in the bottom of my rucksack. I guess somehow the heat and the dark and the bits of old sandwiches work some kind of chemical reaction that brings socks to life. . ."

"Like the first life on earth emerging from the primeval soup!" whispered Polly, awestruck.

"Har har!" jeered Harvey. "Buster's got primeval soup in his rucksack!" Then he remembered what they were up against, and grew quickly serious. "But what are we going to do? That sock's gone rogue! We can't let it rampage all over Smogley!"

"Did you hit it with the antidote, Buster?" asked Cole.

Buster shook his head. "Sorry. The pong was too much for me. I suppose there might be a few drops left in that broken jam jar. I'll go back down and get it. . ."

They all looked towards the hole where the cheese counter had been. Ominous grumbling noises came from below, and they could hear water sloshing and gulping as the sock hauled its vast weight to and fro,

"No," said Polly firmly. "It's too risky."

"Then we'll need more antidote," Buster pointed out.

"There isn't any," she said. "I used up all the ingredients making that jamjarful."

"Then what *are* we going to do?"

"We could wait for the army to arrive," said Harvey. "They'll sort it out."

"How?" demanded Polly. "It's a sock. You can't shoot it. Or you can, but it wouldn't make any difference. If they start firing guns and rockets at it they'll just make it angry, and it's angry enough already. Mind you, I'd be pretty angry if I'd been stuck on Buster's smelly feet every week for PE. . ."

"You're right," said Buster. "It's my sock, so I've

got to deal with it. If the army or any other grown-ups get a look at it they'll soon work out it's mine and I'll be in even more trouble than all the trouble I'm probably in already."

"How will they know it's yours?" asked Polly. "To the untrained eye it's just a giant sock."

"Yes, but it's got my name sewn into it at the top end," said Buster sheepishly. "You know, Mum got this big roll of name-tags printed when I first started school, and there were so many of them that she still sews one into everything I wear; all my shirts and jumpers and trousers and socks. Even my pants have name-tags. . ."

"Har har!" chortled the Quirke Brothers. "Buster's got his name in his pants, *and* there's primeval soup in his rucksack! Har har!"

Buster went bright red. This was getting embarrassing. Luckily, Polly was more interested in saving Smogley than sniggering at other people's y-front-monickering mums. She picked up a cardboard cut-out of a beaming Spudsylvanian cheese-maid and walloped each Quirke Brother round the head with it.

"Ow!" they complained.

"Stop mucking about this instant," she ordered. "I want to hear how Buster thinks we're going to get rid of this sock of his."

The Quirke Brothers stifled a last few giggles and turned to face Buster. Polly kept the cheese-maid handy just in case. "Well, Buster?" she asked politely.

Buster unwrapped a chocolate biscuit that he had found amongst the debris and ate it thoughtfully. "Ooh!" he said suddenly.

"What is it?" they all asked. "Have you had an idea?"

"No, it's this biscuit; it's a really nice minty one. I'll have to tell Mum to put some of these on her shopping list next week. . ."

Polly howled with exasperation as the Quirke Brothers went burrowing off into the wreckage in search of minty biscuits of their own. "Buster! There aren't going to be any shops left for her to shop *at* if we don't sort out your demented sock soon! We need a plan!"

"It's all right," the Quirke Brothers told her, emerging again with handfuls of snacks. "Chocolate is a brain-food; it'll help us think of something."

"We could get an enormous tub full of sock-destroying acid and disguise it as a big cheesy trainer and lure the sock into it," Cole suggested.

"Or, or, or," said Harvey, "we could just lure it into a giant washing machine and wash it at a too-high temperature. That makes things shrink. We know, 'cos we washed some of Dad's shirts for him when we were trying to earn extra pocket money, and they sort of shrank a bit. They really suit our Action Men, though."

"And where are we going to get a giant washing machine from?" asked Buster, spotting the flaw in Harvey's plan. Then all the chocolate he had eaten took effect and his own brain slipped into gear. "I know! We can't shoot the sock, and it's too squidgy to squash and too socky to drown and probably too wet and cheesy to burn. But maybe it could be eaten!"

"EUGH!"

said Polly.

"We're full," said Harvey and Cole hurriedly.

"No, not by us," Buster explained. "I mean by Hamish. He eats more or less anything; Linzi Moss was telling me how he scoffed her dad's slippers last time she had him home. I bet he'd eat a giant sock. All we have to do is get the two of them together somehow!"

Polly and the Quirke Brothers looked at each other. "It's a long shot," said Harvey softly, "but it might just work."

Buster thought hard. The problem was, Hamish was at the far end of town somewhere; probably still snoozing in the park. How could they persuade the monster sock to go there? "We need cheese," he decided. "That's obviously what the sock likes best. It's been soaking up cheesy foot-odour for so long that it's developed a taste for it."

"Well, all the cheese in this place has been scoffed already," Polly said.

"There must be some left somewhere," Buster told her. "Come on, everyone start looking."

They prowled the shattered aisles, but there was no sign of anything remotely cheesy. The sock had even eaten all the cheese-and-onion crisps. Buster was just getting ready to give up when he noticed a small metal door in the back wall – a door labelled STOREROOM and STAFF ONLY, and underneath that, CHEESE AND DAIRY PRODUCTS. "Over here!" he shouted, and the others crowded close behind him as he pushed it open.

They found themselves in a room lined with huge steel fridges. A damaged neon light stuttered and buzzed on the ceiling, splashing big scary shadows around. "Hooray! The sock hasn't been in here!" said Cole.

"These fridge doors must be smell-proof," Polly guessed. "I don't suppose it knows all this is here."

Buster opened the nearest fridge, and looked in at a towering stack of cheddar. "Not smelly enough," he said.

"There's gorgonzola in this one," said Harvey, opening another. "That's pretty smelly. . ." As he spoke, they felt the deep, rumbling snarl of the sock tremble upwards through the floor beneath their feet as it scented cheese.

Buster shut the fridge door and leaned against it. "Right! Now we know how we're going to get the sock to follow us to Hamish!"

"But where is Hamish?" asked Polly.

"I bet he's still in the park," said Buster.

"But you can't be sure of that."

"Oh yes I can!" Buster explained. "He's probably still snoozing, the lazy lump. You and Cole had better go down there. Take Harvey's bike. Cole can show you where Hamish is sleeping. When you hear the sock coming, prod him with a branch or something and wake him up."

"I still don't understand how we're going to make the sock go to the park," said Harvey, unbuckling his cycle helmet and handing it to Polly.

"That's our job," said Buster, leading them back out of the cheese-store and carefully shutting the door behind them. They could feel the floor tremble as the sock sloshed about down below: it had caught a faint whiff of cheese, and was trying to work out where it had come from.

As Polly climbed aboard Harvey's bike and went wobbling off after Cole, Buster hurried over to where the super-de-luxe pedal-car lay and dragged it clear of the debris, sweeping assorted pasta shapes off its bonnet. Beckoning Harvey over he said, "This is our getaway car. Reckon you can drive it?"

"But it's a pedal car! It's for little tiny kids!"

"It'll have to do," said Buster. Harvey nodded uncertainly and climbed into the car. It was much too small for him, and the axles groaned a bit as he settled himself on the seat, but it held his weight, and he started doing experimental circuits of the baked beans display, shouting, "Vroom! Vroooom!"

Buster hurried back into the cheese-store. He was about to open the second fridge and grab some gorgonzola when he noticed another, even bigger fridge near the back of the room. *Spudsylvanian Stinkhorn*, said a yellow warning notice on the door. *Danger! Smelly Cheese Hazard. Protective garments must be worn.*

Gas masks and rubber gloves hung from pegs beside the fridge. Quickly, Buster pulled some on, then slid back the bolts and swung the steel door open. As the fridge light flicked on he gave a rubbery, gas-mask-muffled gasp. In front of him, leaking wisps of greenish vapour, lay the biggest cheese he had ever seen; a splodgy white disc the size of a tractor wheel with pale mould growing from its rind.

"Wow!" he said.

0.2 seconds later the floor of the storeroom erupted into a storm of flying rubble as Buster's giant sock came bursting up through it, lured from its sewery lair by the stench of the super-cheese.

"Waaargh!"

said Buster. The whole room tilted, and the wheel of Spudsylvanian Stinkhorn was thrown out of the fridge and began to roll towards the open door. The sock made a lunge for it, but most of its knitted body was still wedged in the floor and it bellowed in rage as the cheese rolled past it and out into the supermarket. Buster grabbed a second gas mask for Harvey and then ran after it, chucking lumps of gorgonzola into the sock's ragged mouth to distract it. He soon caught up with the Stinkhorn, and bowled it towards the baked beans display, where Harvey stopped the pedal car and held his nose. "What's that smell?"

There wasn't time to explain. Buster chucked the

spare gas mask to him and grabbed hold of the huge cheese. Harvey quickly got the idea and put the mask on, while Buster clambered on to the back of the little car. The front wheels tilted up in the air, almost spilling Buster and his cheesy burden off the back, and Harvey's feet flailed uselessly at the pedals. "Vroom! Vrooom!" he shouted, but it didn't help.

Behind them, the storeroom crumpled and disintegrated and the giant sock gave a furious roar as it shook itself free of the rubble.

"Buster! Do something!" wailed Harvey, wishing the pedal car didn't come complete with wing mirrors, because they gave him a perfect view of the killer sock as it oozed its way along the aisles towards him.

Buster heaved the cheese up over Harvey's head. He had been planning to try and rest it on the bonnet, where its weight would force the car's front end back on to the ground, but halfway there he lost his grip and the cheese slipped out of his hands. There was a loud squelch as it landed on Harvey –

"VROOM! VROOM! ERK!"

Engulfed in cheese, Harvey lurched forward, and as the car's centre of balance shifted, the front wheels hit the lino. His feet were still pumping the pedals, and Buster almost fell off again as the car lurched forward, zooming out of the sock's reach just in time.

"Gfffnllbrrgfh!" protested Harvey, his head completely hidden inside the Spudsylvanian Stinkhorn. He looked as if he was wearing a

cheese hat several sizes too big for him. Luckily he still had his gas mask on underneath, protecting him from the hideous pong, but he couldn't hear much, and he couldn't see anything at all.

"Just drive!" screamed Buster, risking a glance over his shoulder and glimpsing the great grey shape of the sock in hot pursuit. Then he realized what

Harvey's muffled complaint had meant. Blinded by cheese, the boy couldn't see where he was going, and the pedal car was careering towards a huge pyramid of breakfast-cereal boxes, a display which had somehow escaped the sock's first onslaught.

"Go left! Left!" Buster shouted.

"Mggff?"

The car swung to the right, and cannoned straight into the display. For a moment Buster's world dissolved in a snapping, crackling, popping tornado of cereal.

"Oooh! Ow! Youch!"

he shouted, as family-size boxes of Choc-o-Plops and Shreddy-Brek bounced off his bonce. Then they were through to the other side, and when he looked back he saw that the sock had paused to root about in the heap of fallen boxes, as if confused by the way its prey had vanished into the stack.

"Mnnbfl!" said Harvey.

Buster tugged a miniature variety-pack of Golden Nuggets out of his hair and knocked on the top of the cheese, "You're doing fine!" he told Harvey, shouting as loudly as he could to make himself heard. "Keep going straight ahead!"

The shattered automatic doors at the entrance to

the supermarket stood open, and with Buster yelling, "Left a bit... Right a bit..." and Harvey pedalling for dear life, the car went shooting out into the car park and swerved towards the footpath which led to Dancers Road.

A few metres behind it, like a huge, grey, hairy snake, the rogue sock came slithering in cheese-crazed pursuit.

8. THE SMOGLEY EYE

It was turning into a strange afternoon in Smogley. Half the town were piling into their cars and heading for the countryside, terrified by the rumours of earth-tremors and a monster on the loose, while the other half seemed to believe the mayor's claim that everything was under control and were calmly making their way down to the canal-side for the Millennium Gala.

At Ashtree Close, Buster's mum was starting to get quite worried about him. She was used to him scarpering off to the park of a Saturday morning, but he didn't usually leave so early, or stay out so long. So she was quite relieved when the doorbell rang early that afternoon. "That'll be Buster, home for lunch," she thought, putting her book on the archaeology of Smogshire aside and hurrying to the front door. "Wherever have you been, you little monkey?" she said, opening the door – and stopped short, because it wasn't Buster standing on the doorstep, but Nutley Wagstaff, dressed in his full mayoral regalia and surrounded by clerks, aldermen and TV crews.

"Are you Erica Bayliss?" he asked.

"Yes," admitted Buster's mum.

"TV personality Erica Bayliss?"

"That's right," said Buster's mum, wondering if this was another one of Buster's practical jokes.

The mayor of Smogley looked her up and down, as if she wasn't quite what he had been expecting. "Oh well," he sighed. "You'll have to do."

Nutley Wagstaff had been having a very trying few hours. Not only was the mystery beast still on the loose, spreading panic and flattening supermarkets, but he had just taken a telephone call from Dwight Placebo. The hunky actor had heard rumours of trouble afoot in Smogley and was cancelling his plans to attend the afternoon's festivities! With the grand opening looming, Mr Wagstaff needed a TV personality fast, and the closest thing Smogley could provide was Erica Bayliss.

"No time to explain," he barked. "Go and get some smarter clothes on and come with me. You're going to be opening the new Smogley Docks experience."

"Me?" Buster's mum had read about the redevelopment in the papers, and she didn't really approve. When she had been Buster's age the old docks had been her favourite place, and she had spent happy afternoons making Fake Auntie Pauline play cops and robbers there. She liked them the way they used to be, as tumbledown warehouses, and she didn't think she wanted to see them turned into wine bars and art galleries and expensive apartments. She certainly didn't want to open them! "But I've never done anything like that..." she told Nutley Wagstaff.

"As long as you can cut a ribbon and smile at the same time, you'll be fine. Now hurry up. We've got to be at the canal-side for two thirty. You can bring a couple of guests if you like, but you'd better make it sharpish. . ."

Buster's mum wondered if she could refuse, but the mayor and his friends didn't look like the sort of people who would take no for an answer. She hurried back into the house and quickly telephoned Polly's mum, Fake Auntie Pauline. "Hello, F – I mean, Pauline," she said, "I suppose you've not seen Buster?"

"I haven't," replied her friend, sounding crackly and disapproving at the other end of the line. "He's dragged Polly off to play some silly game: she left a note for me. It's really most inconvenient. . ."

"Sorry, Pauline," said Buster's mum, not wanting to listen to another lecture about what a bad influence Buster was. "The thing is, I've just been asked to open the new Smogley Docks, and I wondered if you and Tim could find Buster and bring him along. You'll all be my guests. Polly too, obviously."

There was a crisp little pause as Pauline thought this over. "You're opening the new Smogley Docks Experience?" she asked. "You? And we'll be your guests? Will there be a VIP enclosure? And champagne? And canapés?"

"Yes, of course," said Buster's mum, not liking to admit that she wasn't entirely sure what a canapé was. "But do try and bring Buster, won't you?"

"Yes, yes, yes," said Fake Auntie Pauline, imagining herself rubbing shoulders with a galaxy of minor celebrities and getting her picture in the *Bunchester Evening Echo*. "And I have a wonderful new hat that will be perfect for the occasion. . ."

"Two for two thirty," shouted Buster's mum, cutting off Fake Auntie Pauline's description of her new hat before she had got further than the feathers on the top. "Don't be late, and bring Buster and Polly!"

She slammed the phone down and hurried upstairs to change, pursued by the impatient tootling of the mayor's car-horn.

It was a day of traffic jams and road-closures, of queues and tooting and policemen waving people away from streets blocked by mysteriously uprooted lamp-posts. Polly and Cole found their way to the park by sideways and twittens, and now and then they had to pedal along a path with signs that said NO CYCLING, something that Polly had never done before. She was a bit nervous about breaking the law, but she told herself that this was an emergency and the usual rules didn't apply. Even so, she was feeling rather daring by the time they reached the park.

They had just pedalled through the main gate

when a strange trilling noise started coming from somewhere under Polly's jacket. It took her a moment to recognize the weeble of the new mobile phone her parents had given her for a birthday present. She pulled it out of her pocket and answered it, then held it well away from her ear as her mother's voice came crackling out, so fast and shrill that it sounded like the sort of phone-call people only get in cartoons.

"Polly!" chirped the phone urgently, "Come home this minute, you naughty girl! You know we don't like you playing outside unsupervised! And anyway, something really exciting has happened; your Auntie Erica is opening the new Smogley Docks Experience and we're all going as special guests and you're to come home immediately and get ready! And Erica says she wants Buster there too, although Heaven knows why, he'll only spoil it. . ."

"Mum!" shouted Polly, finally managing to get a word in edgeways. "I can't! I'm really busy!"

"But Polly—"

Polly sighed. There was no point trying to explain what was happening. She shouted over her mother's voice, "Sorry, Mummy, the signal's going!" then made some crackly, swooshy noises and switched the phone off.

Cole was looking at her with admiration. She

slipped the phone back into her pocket, feeling rather pleased with herself. "Come on!" she said.

The lawns, the tennis courts, the playground, the walk around the pond were all deserted: even the park-keeper's hut stood empty, although Mr Crust had taken the trouble to pin a notice to the door announcing, CLOSED DUE TO RAMPAGING MONSTER. Cole led the way down the slope into the Dell, where the trampled earth and gnawed trees made Polly realize that Hamish had grown just as enormous as Buster's sock. She hoped he hadn't turned just as fierce, and started to get a little nervous as Cole stopped his bike and climbed off, motioning for her to follow and keep quiet. They crept on foot through the dense undergrowth. Cole crouched behind a bush and beckoned for her to come and stand beside him, then pulled a leafy branch aside to reveal. . .

Nothing. Sunshine, breaking through the thinning fog, slanted down through the trees to make puddles of shadow and light on the wide circle of flattened foliage where Hamish had been sleeping, but of the hamster himself there was no sign.

"Maybe the potion's worn off like you said it would," said Cole. "Maybe he's gone back to normal size and he's hiding somewhere. . ."

"And maybe not," said Polly. "I knew Buster hadn't

thought his stupid plan through! Hamish has woken up and wandered off!"

At that moment the creak and crash of a falling tree came echoing down the wooded slopes of the Dell, then another and another.

They ran back to their bikes and half rode, half pushed them through the woods, following the wake of overturned trees and scrabbled footprints that Hamish had left as he scrambled up on to the grassy ridge above the Dell. They emerged from the treeline just in time to see Hamish hurrying down the far side of the ridge, scrambling through gardens and over the collapsing roofs of houses.

"We've got to get him back!" yelled Polly. "He's the only thing that can save Smogley from the monster sock!"

"Looks like he's making for the canal!" Cole said. "I wonder why?"

"Look!"

Polly was pointing towards the new Smogley Docks. There, in the hazy sunlight, still half-hidden by the fading fog, something big and circular towered high into the air. It looked as if God had taken one of the wheels off His bike and left it propped there on the canal-side.

"The Smogley Eye!" whispered Polly.

"So that's what my mum was on about," murmured

Cole. "It's not a giant furry seal at all; it's a giant *Ferris wheel!*"

With so many bigger, hairier things to think about, Polly had completely forgotten the goings on at Smogley Docks. Now she remembered seeing the reports on the local news. There had been models and drawings of the new development, and at the heart of it had been this huge white Ferris wheel, with futuristic-looking glass pods that you could go for rides in, giving you a view across the rooftops of Smogley all the way down to the sea at Smogmouth, forty-five kilometres away. It was an amazing feat of engineering, and the mayor had proudly announced that it would be the biggest ferris wheel in the whole world. To Hamish the Hamster, whose favourite pastime had been running round and round in his hamster-wheel, it must simply look like a dream come true.

Fake Auntie Pauline was so eager to get to Smogley Docks that she had not bothered going to look for Polly and Buster. Oddly enough, she had had no interest at all in attending the opening gala before – a nasty, vulgar do, she had called it – but now that she was going to be in the VIP enclosure she could hardly wait to get there. "If Polly would rather play silly games with Buster than be seen with all the best people in Smogley, that's her business," she told Fake Uncle Tim, as she dragged him out of the house. "I'm certainly not going to let her make me late. . ."

"But. . ." said Fake Uncle Tim, who was a little worried about his missing daughter.

"No buts, Timothy," his wife replied. "Polly knows she shouldn't go out without permission. She'll be disappointed when she finds she's missed such a glittering occasion, but let it be a lesson to her."

Now they were making their way towards Smogley Docks in Fake Uncle Tim's car, and Fake Auntie Pauline was sighing and checking her watch every two minutes and trying not to notice the strange, uncomfortable sensations that were coming from beneath her lovely new hat. It felt almost as if something were moving about in there. . . She wondered if she should take it off and have a look, but she didn't want to spoil her hair-do, so she just pressed it down slightly more firmly and tried to take her mind off it by complaining about the snarled-up traffic clogging Dancers Road. "Take a short cut, Tim!" she said at last. "Go on! Turn off here and cut round the back of the gasworks. . ."

Fake Uncle Tim knew that it was easiest just to do as he was told when Pauline was in this mood, so he swung the car out of the line of traffic into a quiet side street.

"There!" said Fake Auntie Pauline. "That's better! Now – what's *that*?"

Another vehicle was speeding up the street towards them, ignoring the one-way signs and Fake Uncle Tim's frantic toots. He had to swerve up on to the pavement to avoid it as it went wobbling past amid the sounds of high-speed pedalling and someone shouting "Left! Left! No, right!"

"That was Buster Bayliss!" gasped Fake Auntie Pauline. "In a gas mask! And a boy with a cheese on his head! In a pedal car!"

But Fake Uncle Tim wasn't listening. He was more interested in the thing that was following Buster: a huge, grey shape that came spilling around the corner of the street and hauled itself towards him, its hairy bulk filling the windscreen, its huge, black mouth widening to swallow the car.

"Eeeeeeek!"

shriek ed Fake Auntie Pauline.

"Don't worry, dear!" Fake Uncle Tim told her, slamming his foot down on the accelerator. The car seemed to be rushing through a knitted tunnel, soggy, cheese-clogged fur pressed close against the windows, but there was a gleam of light ahead, and after a few seconds they emerged into daylight again. Fake Uncle Tim stopped the car and they sat in silence, watching in the rear-view mirror as the monstrous shape dragged itself to the far end of the street and turned left on to Dancers Road.

"What on earth was that?" asked Fake Uncle Tim.

"That," said his wife, "was something to do with Buster Bayliss."

"How do you know?"

"It had his name-tag sewn into it. I saw it quite distinctly."

"Would you like to go home, Pauline?" asked Fake Uncle Tim. "I mean, if that thing's on the loose it might not be altogether wise to go to the gala. And poor Polly might be. . ."

"Not go?" Fake Auntie Pauline was incredulous. "Of course we'll go! I'm not going to let Buster Bayliss's hooliganism stop me hobnobbing with the mayor and his guests!"

Fake Uncle Tim nodded, peering out through sock-smeared windows at the car, which was now plastered with sewage and melted cheese and bits of fluff. He wound his window down and sniffed, then wound it up again very quickly. "I think we'd better walk the rest of the way," he said.

*

"Left a bit! Right a bit! Left! Left! LEFT!"

"Mngnff! Frrbble fb!"

The purloined pedal car went hurtling along the

pavements of Dancers Road, pedestrians throwing themselves out of its path, bewildered people peering out of car windows as it passed, the sock slooshing along behind, knocking the awnings off all the shops. "Left!" screamed Buster, and Harvey spun the steering wheel, the car tilting over on to two wheels as it screeched round a corner into Hawthorne Avenue. The sock wasn't so good at cornering; it had to pause and heave itself around before it came on, and so the boys gained a few precious metres, but Buster could still feel its hot, socky breath on the back of his neck as Harvey pedalled into the park.

Through the scented garden for the blind they went, Buster's windmilling arms knocking the tops off all the flowers beside the path as he struggled to keep his balance on the back of the car – but that didn't matter, because the sock was still on their tail, and the flowers were flattened seconds later anyway. Over the football pitch, round the pond, through the children's playground ("Duck!" yelled Buster just in time, as they shot through the gap beneath the plank-swing with millimetres to spare). Then they were rattling down the slope into the Dell, off the path and into a slalom-course of abandoned fridges and hamster-nibbled trees.

"Left!" blurted Buster. "Right! Left a bit! Tree dead ahead! Go right! Right! I mean left!"

A moment later a series of strange but interesting noises echoed around the Dell:

Screeeeeeep! Aaaaaaaaargh! **STONK!**
Yip! *Ooof!* Thwelch! Wooarbaargh!
PLUD! Flif–flif–flif–flif... *SPLADOTCH!*

"Buster?" It was Polly's voice, and when Buster opened his eyes he saw that it was coming from Polly herself, who had just ridden into the Dell aboard Harvey Quirke's bike. Curiously, the world seemed to be upside down, and Buster spent a couple of seconds wondering where Polly had learned to ride a bike head downwards. Then he gradually realized that the world was right-way-up after all and that it was he who was the upside-down one.

"Ow!" he said, trying to work out what had happened. He thought back over the series of interesting noises and gradually worked out what they had all meant.

<u>Those Interesting Noises Explained In Full</u>

1. **Screeeeeeeep!** The sound of a pricey pedal-car applying its brakes and skidding full tilt towards an abandoned fridge-freezer.

2. **Aaaaaaaaaaaaaargh!** Reaction of Buster Bayliss to the above.

3. **STONK!** The noise of a pedal car's front bumper meeting a fridge door at speed.

4. **"Yip!" "Ooooof!"** The sounds of a) Buster being hurled off his perch on the back of the car and b) Harvey being jolted against the steering wheel.

5. **Thwelch!** The distinctive sound made when 200 kg of the World's Smelliest Cheese is dislodged from someone's head by the force of a pedal-car/fridge collision.

6. **"Wooarbaargh!"** Buster's comment, as he sailed up into the air.

7. **PLUD!** The noise he made as he hit the ground (luckily a pile of giant hamster droppings cushioned his fall).

8. **Flif-flif-flif-flif. . .** This is the rather calming whistle that a lump of Spudsylvanian Stinkhorn makes as it turns end over end in mid-air. . .

9. **SPLADOOOTCH!** The not-at-all-calming noise that it made as it landed smack in the face of Cole Quirke, who had come pedalling into the Dell just ahead of Polly.

Right, that's that sorted out, thought Buster, standing up and checking his arms and legs to make sure that they were all still where he had left them. Then he took a quick look around the Dell. Polly was looking anxiously at him, and Cole was staggering about going, "Agck! Gabargle! Spluff! Churk! Boggg!" as he tried to scrape the whiffy cheese off his face. After a few seconds he collapsed, overcome by the pong. "Cole!" shouted Harvey, running to help and pulling his gas mask off so he could make himself heard. Almost at once he too was overcome by the fumes of the cheese that was still plastered in his hair, and he fell over unconscious beside his brother.

"No sign of Hamish, then?" said Buster, cautiously taking his own gas mask off and looking around in the hope of spotting the hamster's enormous furry bod among the trees.

Polly shook her head. She usually looked faintly worried when Buster was about, but he had never seen her look quite as concerned as this, and he knew that something had gone pretty disastrously wrong with his luring-giant-sock-into-jaws-of-monster-hamster plan.

"Hamish is awake," Polly explained. "He's on the move again, heading for Smogley Docks."

Buster thought fast, smoke pouring from his ears as his brain worked overtime. "We'll have to follow him there. Take the cheese with us and hope the sock follows. . ."

"What cheese?" asked Polly.

Buster could see what she meant. Steaming gobbets of Spudsylvanian Stinkhorn lay scattered all across the Dell, clinging to every available tree, fridge and Quirke Brother. It would take hours to gather it all up, and they didn't have hours. They didn't even have seconds. An angry roar made the ground shake, and a tidal wave of greyish wool came surging towards them, flattening the trees which stood in its path and hurling leaves and twigs and startled birds into the air above it.

There was no time to do anything but run. Buster and Polly each grabbed a comatose Quirke Brother by one foot and, dragging the dazed and burbling boys behind them, stumbled away as fast as they could.

Behind them, the rogue sock rolled into the Dell, engulfing fridges, freezers and the wreck of the pedal car. The smell of cheese was strong here, and it ignored Buster and Polly and started feeling about with its huge, blunt snout and nudging bits of Stinkhorn into its mouth. They could still hear it rooting about down there as they reached the top of the ridge, and Buster saw for the first time the broad furrow of destruction that Hamish had cut through gardens and houses as he headed towards the Smogley Eye.

"Ooops!" he said.

"We've got to do something, Buster," Polly urged him. "Our mummies are down there at the Smogley Docks Experience!"

"Mine isn't."

"Yes she is! My mummy told me your mummy was going to be doing the official opening! If we don't think of something, she might be squashed by Hamish!"

Buster thought hard, but he couldn't think of a new plan, so he decided to stick to the one he had. "The sock. . . If we can make it follow us to the docks maybe it'll distract Hamish long enough for everybody to get away. . ." He looked back down the hill. The monster sock seemed to have finished hunting for bits of cheese amongst the brambles and was snuffling about trying to pick up the scent that the Stinkhorn-spattered Quirkes had left as Buster and Polly hauled them to safety. As Buster watched, it found their trail, and the frayed fur bristled upright on its back as it uttered a howl of cheese-lust and began pushing its way towards him up the slope.

103

"Come on!" he shouted, heaving Harvey to his feet and shaking him until the bewildered boy was just about able to walk. Polly did the same with Cole, and together the four of them went blundering down into the hamster-trashed streets between the park and the canal-side.

9. SOCK-ECLIPSE NOW

Erica Bayliss, Buster's mum, wasn't used to opening things. At least, she knew she was all right at opening cupboards and jam jars and packets of pasta, but she had never opened a new Docks Experience complete with giant Ferris wheel before, and she was starting to get rather nervous.

"It'll be a doddle, love," the mayor assured her as they turned on to the new canal-side walk in his long, black official car. "All you have to do is say, "I declare this wonderful Millennium Dockland Experience open!" or some sort of old rubbish like that, and then you and me and me lady wife here will take the first ride on the Smogley Eye."

"Huh!" said his wife, a thin, disapproving woman who sat on the other side of him. "You'll not get me up there! Nasty dangerous-looking thing it is, if you ask me!"

"You'll have a go, and like it!" the mayor told her crossly. "How many more times do I have to explain it to you, Myrtle. The Smogley Eye is the greatest project ever created in this town, and it's perfectly safe."

"I wish Buster was here," said Buster's mum to herself, looking out of the car's tinted windows at the towering shapes of the old warehouses which lined either side of the canal, now converted into fashionable coffee shops, expensive luxury apartments and an art gallery called Smogley:Modern which was showing a ground-breaking exhibition of fluff sculptures from all over the world. A large crowd had gathered on the posh new cobbled walkways that stretched along the canal-side, and even more were crammed into the plaza where the gigantic Smogley Eye stood waiting. She wondered if Fake Auntie Pauline had succeeded in dragging Buster and her daughter away from whatever game they had been so wrapped up in and managed to get them here, but she couldn't see any of them watching her as the car slowed to a halt in front of a bunting-draped podium and the mayor's chauffeur opened the passenger door and helped her out.

"Hooray!" shouted the crowd, a bit half-heartedly, as they realized that hunky Dwight Placebo hadn't turned up after all and that his place was to be taken by Erica Bayliss, who most of them had never even heard of. The mayor took off his three-cornered mayoring hat and waved it graciously to acknowledge the scattering of bored applause, but Mrs Bayliss couldn't help feeling a bit embarrassed as she followed him up the steps of the podium. Overhead, dozens of helicopters clattered to and fro. At first she'd assumed that they were TV people, but now, as one passed quite low over the towering Ferris wheel, she noticed that they were army helicopters. And those big, camouflage-pattern shapes drawn up beyond the new warehouse apartments – were they really tanks? "What on earth is going on?" she asked.

"Nothing, my dear! Simple precautions!" the mayor reassured her, pulling her with him towards the cluster of microphones at the front of the podium.

"But all these soldiers and tanks and things—"

The mayor shoved his big red face close to Mrs Bayliss, covering the nearest microphones with his hat in case they picked up what he was about to say. "Between you and me, love, there's a wild animal of some sort loose in Smogley. A bear, or possibly an elephant. Or a giant furry snake. None of the witnesses can agree. The Royal Smogshire Fusiliers are here to deal with it."

"A wild animal!" Mrs Bayliss looked alarmed. "Is it dangerous? I must go and find Buster! He might be in danger—"

She turned and started to hurry back towards the steps, but the mayor had a firm grip on her arm. "The main thing is, we don't want to cause any disruption to the opening ceremonies, do we? Could cause irreparable damage to the tourist trade if people get the idea that Smogley's infested with giant hairy snakes."

"But Buster. . ."

"You can go and find him after you've done the opening, all right?" The mayor turned to the increasingly puzzled crowd and gave them his best impression of a cheery smile. "Ladies and gentlemen, boys and girls," he announced. "I'd like to welcome you all to this very special and posh occasion: the opening of Smogley's very own, slightly delayed, Millennium Project!"

"Hoorah!" went the crowd, uncertainly.

"Where's Dr Doug?" shouted a teenage girl.

"Sadly, Mr Placebo can't be with us today," the mayor said.

"Boooooooo!"

called the crowd, the echoes of their disappointment bouncing from the plate-glass windows of the brand new shops and galleries and luxury warehouse-apartments.

"However," the mayor shouted, holding up his hands to call for quiet, "I am very pleased to present Smogley's very own, home-grown TV celebrity, the new face of Britain's third most popular archaeology programme, *Dig This!* presenter Ms Erica Bayliss!"

"Who?" said the crowd.

"We want Dr Doug!" wailed the teenager, and all her friends agreed.

The mayor steered Mrs Bayliss to the microphone. "Well, get on with it, then," he said.

Buster's mum gave a nervous gulp, and the microphones picked it up and sent it booming out of all the loudspeakers, making some naughty members of the crowd titter. "Um, well," she said, gazing awkwardly out at a sea of expectant faces. "Ah, the thing is, I'm not used to public speaking, and I'd just like to say. . . "Eeeeek!"

"Funny speech," said the crowd, turning to look at each other in surprise. "Nice and short, though." Then some of them had the sense to look at what Ms Bayliss was pointing at; something that was lumbering towards them along the canal-side.

"*Eeeeeeek!*"

they squealed, and began to surge towards the exits.

"It looks like some sort of rodent!" gasped Buster's mum. "But it's enormous! Twenty-five metres high at least!"

A helicopter gunship swooped low overhead, drowning out the mayor's reply with the dull thwup-thwup-thwup of its rotor blades*. The camouflage-clad soldier in the helicopter's open door was armed with a dart-gun loaded with elephant tranquillizers and fired dart after dart down at the monster – but to Hamish they were just a minor irritation, like being nibbled by a very old gnat that has left its false teeth at home. He reared up on his hind legs and took a swipe at the annoying helicopter, knocking it down into the waters of the Smogley-Bunchester canal.

*And a good thing too, since he was using words which you're not supposed to know.

"Not the canal! We've just had it cleaned! There's stickleback in there!" wailed Nutley Wagstaff, as rainbow-patterns of leaking fuel spread from the smashed machine. "And no boating allowed!" he added, as the helicopter's crew paddled away from the wreck in a rubber dinghy. Then something else caught his attention. "Oh no! The apartments! My beautiful luxury warehouse apartments! Somebody do something!"

It was too late. Hamish had lost balance when he swiped at the helicopter, and now he went blundering sideways, completely demolishing the nearest block of warehouses. Alarmed by the crash of falling masonry, he leaped backwards, and his rear end slammed into the front of Smogley:Modern, smashing it to pieces. Priceless bits of fluff went scattering across the canal-side, pursued by wailing artists. Hamish scrambled up on to the ruins of an expensive American coffee shop and batted a couple more helicopters out of the way.

"He looks as if he's having fun," said Buster's mum.

"This is a disaster!" wailed the mayor.

The damaged helicopters made emergency landings, and, as their frightened pilots jumped out and joined the panic-stricken crowds rushing away from the canal, the rest pulled away to a safe distance. Hamish the Hamster sat amid the rubble for a few seconds, nose twitching, then came prowling towards the podium.

"Run!" wailed Mrs Bayliss.

There was no way down. The podium steps had been demolished by the fleeing crowds. The only escape route was off the back of the podium and into one of the pods of the slowly turning Smogley Eye.

The mayor, the mayoress and Buster's mum all scrambled aboard, and the wheel had taken them up about fifteen metres before they realized that they had made a really, really bad mistake. The wheel shuddered and groaned on its axles as two hundred tonnes of giant hamster scrambled playfully into position between the spokes. A moment later Buster's mum and her companions felt their pod begin to move backwards, slowly at first but then faster and faster.

It was round about then that Buster and Polly arrived, forcing a path for themselves through the fleeing crowds with the help of the cheesy-smelling Quirke Brothers. Running out on to the debris-strewn cobbles they gawped in amazement at the whirling wheel. Hamish was obviously having the time of his life as he raced along, big pink feet shoving the pods by beneath him, nose twitching, tail a-jiggle. He seemed to have no idea of the chaos he was causing – and no idea either that the Royal Smogshire Fusiliers were about to put a permanent stop to his fun.

A trio of tanks trundled into position quite close to where Buster and the others stood, and the officer in charge popped out of the lid of the leading one and shouted to the other commanders, "All right, chaps; twelve rounds rapid fire at Johnny giant hamster. On my command. . ."

"No!" shouted Buster in desperation. "I've got to take him back to school. . ."

"You'll blow up the Ferris wheel!" screamed Polly. "And there are people aboard!"

Buster hadn't noticed that until she mentioned it. Now, peering at the racing wheel, he noticed that three figures were clinging on for dear life inside one of the pods, and each time it flashed by he could hear them going, "Aaaargh! Help! Let us off!"

"I think that's my mum!" he gasped.

Polly scampered to the wheel, scrambled up on to the sagging podium and spread her arms wide, protecting Hamish from the guns of the tanks. The tank commander pulled out a megaphone and pointed it at her. "Now stand aside, little girl," he ordered.

"No!" shouted Polly.

"Polly!" yelled Buster, afraid that the soldiers

would blow her up along with the wheel and the hamster and his mum. But just then a cold, dark shadow fell across him and spread across the cobbles and out over the waters of the canal like an oil slick. The glints of sunlight on the whizzing pods of the Smogley Eye went out, and the men in the turrets of the waiting tanks looked round in confusion.

Buster's rogue sock towered into the sky above the ruined warehouses, eclipsing the sun.

"Crikey!" shouted the tank commander, forgetting to put down his megaphone. "What the devil's that? It looks like some kind of prehistoric glove-puppet..."

Meanwhile, Hamish the Hamster had also noticed the new arrival. His big pink nose twitched harder than ever as he detected the cheesy pong of sock. He liked that smell. It reminded him of all the parental socks and slippers he had nibbled over the years. He jumped off the wheel, and as he did so he must have caught some vital bit of the mechanism with his hind-leg. There was an ominous crack, an unpleasant creak, an expensive-sounding ker-plingg, and the Smogley Eye broke free of its moorings and went rolling off along the canal-side. Pods snapped off and flew this way and that, some bursting in glittery explosions of glass as they hit the cobbles, others hurtling clear across the canal to crash into the luxury warehouse apartments on the opposite bank. "Mum!" wailed Buster, as each one landed, but luckily the pod with his mum and the mayor aboard dropped in the middle of the canal and bobbed safely in the oily water while its dizzy occupants scrambled out and came splashing towards the bank.

Buster started forward to help, but it was difficult to make any headway, because all the people who had just run away from the canal screaming, "Help! Help! A huge hairy hamster!" were now running back shouting, "Help! Help! A horrible woolly something-or-other!" The tanks swivelled their turrets round and fired at the sock, but their shells just punched small, ragged holes in its hide to match the ones Buster's toenails had made when it was ordinary-sock-size. It snarled indignantly and picked the tanks up one by one, tossing them casually aside. The soldiers inside them piled out through their hatches and ran, but the sock wasn't interested in them; it had sniffed out Harvey and Cole.

"Run!" shouted Buster. It was something that he seemed to have been shouting rather a lot today, but this time there was nowhere much to run to, for all the escape routes which had not been blocked by falling art galleries and luxury warehouse apartments were now clogged with upturned tanks. Undeterred, the Quirke Brothers set off anyway, sprinting in circles around and around the ruined shell of the Smogley:Modern with the sock at their heels. Buster looked round at Hamish, who was watching the sock's every move with bright, beady eyes. "Hamish!" he shouted, pointing towards it. "Kill!"

Hamish bared his big front teeth and started to stalk towards the sock. The sock sensed him coming and reared up, momentarily forgetful of the Quirkes.

"RaaaRRRGHHHH!"

it bellowed, echoes bounding to and fro across the canal.

"Eeeeep!"

squeaked Hamish fiercely, and the high-pitched sound shattered all the windows within a half-mile radius that had not already been broken. The two giants lumbered towards each other. "Come on, Hamish!" shouted Polly. "You can do it!"

Hamish sniffed the sock-scented air and bared his huge teeth eagerly. With a shuddering crash the two monsters slammed into each other, heaving back and forth as Hamish tried to nibble the sock and the sock attempted to wrap itself around Hamish. They knocked over the remains of the Smogley Eye, and trod on the visitor centre, scattering mannequins in authentic Victorian dress into the canal. To Buster's delight, Hamish soon began to get the upper paw. He sank his teeth into the sock's smelly wool and started to gnaw, and from the sock's howls it was pretty clear that the battle would soon be over.

Then, without any warning, Hamish disappeared.

10. SOCK HORROR!

Buster blinked and rubbed at his eyes. "What happened?" he shouted. One minute the giant hamster had been happily tucking into a cheese-flavoured sock-snack, the next there had been a sort of blur and he had vanished. "Where'd he go?"

"He didn't go anywhere!" gasped Polly, running over to join him. "Look!"

Down on the cobbles, looking a little bit confused, a perfectly ordinary, hamster-sized hamster was scurrying round in circles.

"The potion's worn off!" cried Buster. "Brilliant!" Then he remembered the sock. It had gone back to chasing the cheesy Quirkes round and round the rubble-heap, and although Hamish's teeth had made a few holes in its heel it seemed quite all right and showed no sign of shrinking. "Oh no!" he groaned. "Of course . . . the sock didn't get a taste of expanding-potion until about twelve hours after the hamster – so it could be another twelve hours before it goes back to sock-size!"

Polly watched critically as the flagging Quirkes started another circuit of the wreckage. "I don't think Harvey and Cole can keep that up for twelve whole hours," she said.

Buster looked about for somebody who could take charge of things. The soldiers had fled, leaving downed helicopters and upturned tanks scattered along the waterfront like toys on a bedroom floor. Mum was climbing up the steps from the canal, looking bedraggled and very dizzy, followed by the mayor and the mayoress, who was saying, "I should have listened to my mother, Nutley! She told me I was making a mistake the day I married you!" There was nobody else in sight. As usual, it was going to be up to Buster to save the day.

"Bother!" he said.

The Quirke Brothers ran past again, looking increasingly tired. Behind them the sock came slithering round the corner of the ruins. If it had been a more intelligent sock it might simply have doubled back and lain in wait for the boys when they came round again, but none of Buster's socks were very bright, and this one could only think of pursuing the wonderful, cheesy scent of the hurtling Quirkes. It was beginning to fray as it heaved its heavy body over the rough rubble, and the sight of the trailing threads that dragged behind it gave Buster an idea.

"Do something!" panted Harvey, starting another lap.

"Quick!" agreed Cole.

Buster hurried towards them, and the next time the sock lumbered past he grabbed one of the rope-thick threads and quickly wrapped it around an iron bollard which jutted out of the cobblestones nearby. Polly hurried to help him tie the knot and the sock slithered on, unaware that it was beginning to unravel in slow, grey, stinking loops.

"Keep going!" Buster and Polly shouted, egging the

Quirke Brothers on. "You can do it! Just a couple more laps!"

The Quirkes put their heads down and ran on, and behind them the sock grew smaller and smaller, slowly turning into a tangled skein of outsize, greyish wool, looped around the ruins like a heap of leftover spaghetti after a particularly nasty school

dinner. At last it realized what was happening, and turned. Opening its ragged mouth in a last terrible roar it hurled itself towards Buster and Polly.

There was no need to shout "Run!" this time; by the time Buster had said "R—" they were both already running. Ahead of them loomed the canal's edge and a long drop into the water; behind them the unravelling sock came hissing and looping and slithering and snarling, opening its mouth wide to swallow and smother them.

"Jump!" shouted Polly, when they were a few metres from the water. "We'll swim for it!"

"I can't swim!" wailed Buster.

"Why ever not?" Even whilst running for her life from enraged footwear Polly managed to sound impatient with him. "You've had swimming lessons at the leisure pool once a week all term!"

"Yes, but I didn't actually learn to swim," panted Buster, now just a metre from the canal's edge and a watery grave. "I was busy mucking about with the polystyrene floats and having water fights. . ."

"Oh, *Buster*!" said Polly.

They turned together, teetering on the very brink of the canal, and the sock raced towards them. But there was not much left of it now; just an enormous toe, and even that unravelled and unravelled and unravelled until all that remained was the open mouth looming over them, and then even that was gone. The fat strand of wool flopped on to the cobblestones and twitched feebly for a moment before lying still.

"Phew!" breathed Polly, prodding the lifeless wool with her toe.

"Phew!" agreed Buster, glancing over his shoulder at the waters of the canal. "See? I didn't need to bother learning to swim after all. . ."

Harvey and Cole were too busy running to realize what had happened, and Buster thought he would let them do a couple more circuits before he told them that the danger was over, just to serve them right for all the trouble their potions and pet hotels had caused. In fact, now that he thought back over his exhausting day, he didn't see why he should *ever* tell them. . . But Polly took pity on them, and next time they went past she called out, "It's all right now! It's all over!"

The Quirke Brothers skidded to a standstill and fell over, gasping for breath. Buster looked around. It *was* all over, but he couldn't quite believe that he was safe. He still half expected to see a giant odour-eater or some ravening underpants come looming over Smogley's shattered roof-tops. But everything stayed calm. On the cobbles near his feet Hamish the Hamster sat nibbling a bit of someone's abandoned sandwich. Buster gathered him up gratefully, and didn't even mind when Hamish used his hands for a toilet. "All right, boy," he said. "You're safe now. . ."

"Buster?"

It was Mum, dripping with canal water and still swaying dizzily from her ride in the out-of-control eye. Mum didn't very often get cross, but Buster could see from the look in her eye that she was about 0.8 seconds away from blowing up. She eyed Hamish suspiciously. "Where did those great hairy animals go?" she asked. "And where did you get that hamster?"

"It's all right, Mum," squeaked Buster. "All those monsters and stuff were nothing to do with me, honest, and there's no connection at all between Hamish and that enormous giant hamster, I mean, how could there be? I wouldn't go around making hamsters grow enormous. Hamish is a school hamster and he . . . er . . . I mean I . . . um . . . oh, pants!"

Too late, he realized that he had blundered into a trap. Now he was going to have to admit to Mum that he had taken charge of a school pet. "Um, er, ah, ermmmm," he burbled, but although his brain grated and hummed no brilliant ideas popped out, and Mum's scowl grew scowlier and scowlier as she started to put two and two together. She was now just 0.4 seconds from detonation! Wistfully, Buster thought of all the fun he'd had being nearly eaten alive by rampaging socks. He would rather face a monster than an angry Mum any day. . .

Then, just as Mum reached 0.1 and steam started to hiss out of her ears, a wonderful thing happened. Fake Cousin Polly said sweetly, "Excuse me, Auntie Erica, but Hamish is with me. I'm looking after him for the weekend." She pulled off her cycle helmet and held it upside down to make a little nest for Hamish, who climbed happily inside and went to sleep.

Buster's Mum still looked suspicious. "But he looks exactly like that creature which just wrecked the Smogley Eye. . ."

"Don't be silly, Mum," said Buster. "Whoever heard of a hamster attacking a Ferris wheel? I think you must have been hallucinating. You're probably just dizzy from your ride. . ."

"Well, hmmm," said Mum, deciding not to explode after all. "Maybe you're right. . . And I think Smogley Docks look much nicer like this anyway, don't you? Come on, Buster. Pauline and Tim are supposed to be around somewhere. I'll see if they'll give us a lift home."

She set off towards the car park, weaving her way between up-turned tanks and embarrassed-looking soldiers who were trying to work out how they'd tell their friends that they'd been defeated by a sock. Buster hung behind for a moment. "Thanks, Polly," he said. "You saved my life."

"I don't know what came over me," she replied. "You deserve a good telling off, after all the trouble you caused. What are you going to do with Hamish now?"

Buster looked thoughtfully at the cycle helmet. Hamish was a comfortable, curled-up ball of fluff in the bottom; if he had had a thinks-bubble it would have been full of hamster-y zzzz's. "I suppose he'll have to go back to the Quirkes," said Buster doubtfully.

"Oh no!" Harvey and Cole were still lying flat on the ground, gathering their strength for the walk home, but they had heard what Polly and Buster were saying and now they both shook their heads in unison, scattering a few last crumbs of cheese. "Not us!" Harvey said firmly. "We're getting out of the pet-minding business. It's much too dangerous. There must be an easier way to make extra pocket money."

"We could put out burning oil rigs," suggested Cole.

"Yes, or build a spaceship that eats Russian and American spaceships, and hold the world to ransom. . ."

"Or just go to Monte Carlo and win squintillions of pounds on the roulade wheel."

"Or. . ."

Buster and Polly decided to leave them to it, but as they followed Buster's mum away towards the main entrance they could still hear Harvey and Cole plotting. They had a feeling that it wouldn't be long before Smogley was shaken by another of the brothers' get-rich-quick schemes.

"It's all right," said Polly as they walked. "I'll keep Hamish safe till Monday morning. I think there's even an old cage in the loft, left over from when Mummy kept guinea pigs."

The car park was full of confused and angry people. Some had managed to find their cars and were now blowing their horns and glaring out through sock-slimed windscreens as they waited for the snarl-up at the exits to clear, others had just found sad little flattened ex-cars, squashed by Hamish's gigantic feet, and they were standing round the crumpled remains angrily demanding compensation and official inquiries. Buster and Polly shoved their way through the crowd until they spotted Buster's mum standing beside a ruined coffee bar, talking to Polly's parents.

"Oh, poo!" they both said at the same moment (and Buster was actually quite impressed, because he'd hardly ever heard Polly swear before).

In all the excitement of the afternoon they had completely forgotten about poor, miniaturized Fluffikins the cat. Now they turned to stare at each other in horror as they realized that Fake Auntie Pauline was wearing her best hat.

They barged their way to where the grown-ups were standing. "I'm sorry, Erica," they heard Fake Auntie Pauline say as they drew near. "We don't have a car with us. We were on the way here when we met a. . . Well, a. . . It was a. . ."

"We had a little accident," said Fake Uncle Tim.

"Well, I'm not walking all the way home," said Mum. "I know: we'll get a lift in the mayor's Mercedes! He's the one who brought me here; he'll just have to take me home again!"

Fake Auntie Pauline had been about to say that the accident she had met with had had Buster's name neatly stitched into it, but at the mention of the mayor she forgot all about it. If there was one thing Fake Auntie Pauline loved it was hobnobbing with important people like Mayors and Archbishops and People Who Once Met the Queen at a Garden Party. Riding home to Acacia Crescent in the Mayoral Merc would almost make up for her disastrous afternoon.

"He's over there!" said Buster helpfully, sneaking a peek at her hat in the hope of finding out whether Fluffikins was still safe inside — but there was no sign of the minute moggie, and now Fake Auntie Pauline was following Mum towards the place where the wet mayor was sitting gloomily in the back of his car. "Let me talk to him, Erica!" she called, pushing in front of her friend.

"Well?" asked Polly frantically, as they hurried after her. "Did you see him?"

Buster shook his head. "Maybe he fell out when she put the hat on. Maybe he's still at your house, being menaced by ants and bullied by bedbugs!"

"And maybe he's still under Mummy's hat, lost in her hair!" whimpered Polly.

"It's a cat-astrophe!" Buster started to say, but thought better of it and turned it into a cough.

There was quite a scrum building up around the mayor's car, as angry Smogleyites demanded explanations for what had happened and refunds of their car park fees, but nobody could stand in the way of Fake Auntie Pauline, who swept towards the Merc like a mayor-seeking missile with Fake Uncle Tim, Polly, Buster and Buster's mum in her wake. "Your Worship!" she said, beaming brightly, and did a curtsey.

The mayor peeked out at her through the tinted windows. He was getting a bit tired of people shouting at him to explain things and resign. Even his wife was busily telling him that he was a disgrace to public office, and had hit him so many times with her handbag that his mayor's hat had been squished all out of shape. So it came as a nice surprise to see Fake Auntie Pauline smiling so adoringly at him. He cautiously wound the window down a crack and said, "Yes?"

"Oh, Your Worship," purred Fake Auntie Pauline, doing another, even deeper curtsey. All around her, angry people stopped shouting about their squashed cars and leaned closer to hear what she was about to say. The photographer from the *Bunchester Evening Echo*, wondering if she was somebody important, raised his camera, just in case.

And in the brief silence, as she wondered what the most genteel way to cadge a lift would be, the people who were standing closest heard a strange sound coming from somewhere inside Fake Auntie Pauline's hat.

"*Miaoow!*" it went, and then,

"*Burp! Burp! Burp! Buuurp!*"

Buster didn't see what happened next because the photographer's flash-gun dazzled him; he just got a vague impression of a lot of surprised milling about and gasping and yowling and miaowing. But he didn't really need to see, because when he finally got home that evening, there was Fake Auntie Pauline's picture on page two of the *Bunchester Evening Echo*, wearing on her head the exploded remains of an expensive hat and a very life-size, very fat and very startled cat.

11. THE RETURN OF THE HAMSTER

"Everybody CALM DOWN!" shouted Miss Ellis on Monday morning, straining to make herself heard over the chatter of 2b. They were a loud lot at the best of times, but today they were absolutely deafening: everybody was swapping stories about the Smogley Docks disaster.

"Our car got squidged flat!"

"The Smogley Eye didn't stop rolling until it was halfway to Smogmouth!"

"Nutley Wagstaff's run off to join the Foreign Legion!"

As loudly as she could, poor Miss Ellis started taking the register. "David Abbot?"

"Here, Miss."

"Millie Ashford?"

"Here, Miss."

"Buster Bayliss?"

Silence fell, the way it does when someone asks the way to Castle Dracula in a Transylvanian pub. Buster's desk was empty, which was pretty normal on a Monday morning, because it was only five minutes since the bell had gone — but today, everyone was on tenterhooks, wondering what would have happened to Hamish the Hamster over the weekend. Would Buster bring him back wearing little splints and a crutch, like Bertie the Budgie? Or wrapped up in bandages, like Edna the Stick Insect? Or would he never return at all?

"Buster Bayliss?" called Miss Ellis wearily, her red biro poised to mark him absent.

Just in time the door burst open and Buster sauntered into the classroom, holding up a cage containing a perfectly happy, perfectly healthy

Hamish. Even Miss Ellis joined in the cheers, and in all the fuss nobody even noticed that the hamster was ever so slightly bigger than before, and that he was in a new cage.

Buster booted his rucksack under his desk and sat down, feeling relieved. Miss Ellis finished the register and started telling everybody about long division or the Tudors or something similar, but he was already drifting away into a comfortable daze that would only lift when the bell went for morning break. Happily, he pondered the events of the weekend, and decided that everything had worked out pretty well. Hamish was safe, the sock was destroyed, Fluffikins was cat-sized again and nobody had been hurt. Even Fake Auntie Pauline's expensive hat had turned out to be covered by hat insurance. Of course, zoologists would be puzzling for ages over exactly what the creatures were that had demolished the new Smogley Docks Experience, but the photographs which he had seen in the papers had been so blurry, and the TV pictures so wobbly, that there was no danger of anybody connecting them with B. Bayliss of 21, Ashtree Close. Some people said it had been a pair of escaped elephants from a circus, others that it had all been a mass hallucination. The *Bunchester Evening News* reckoned it was all a feeble publicity stunt dreamed up by the mayor. One wildlife expert timidly suggested that in one of the pictures the marauding monster looked a teensy bit like a colossal hamster, but all the other scientists just laughed at her.

And so all was well. Lulled by the drone of his teacher's voice, Buster gave a contented sigh, folded his hands behind his head, and started working out how long there was left to go until half term.

He didn't see the small, grey, woolly shape that poked its toe out of the top of his rucksack, sniffed at the air, and then quickly slithered down on to the floor. A faint pong of cheesy feet wafted across the classroom, but that was nothing unusual when 2b were about. Nobody noticed the second of Buster's socks as it slithered swiftly between the legs of their chairs and down through a gap in the floorboards beside the radiator, heading for the warmth and darkness of the school boiler room. . .

THE END?

LOOK OUT FOR

BY PHILIP REEVE

AN EXTRACT...

The lorry had pulled up to the kitchen door and stopped. It was a red lorry with a sort of yellow splash painted on the side and the single word SCOFFCO. The driver's door opened and out hopped two burly figures in bovver boots and gingham frocks. Buster recognized them at once: they were Pansy and Petunia. Miss Burtle and Poppy hurried with them into the canteen. Buster crouched beside one of the scraggy little trees that stood at the front of the school and watched as they began to carry big crates out of the kitchen and load them aboard the lorry.

"Weird!" he whispered.

"You're right, lad," said the tree. "Now get off my foot!"